"What's happening to us?" Sol asked, his body trembling all over, his pulse racing out of control.

"I don't know," Mariah whispered. She was pinned by his body, by his searching gaze. "I feel so—strange."

"Help me up," he said, and his fingers sought hers. Their wedding bands connected, and their vows were suddenly there between them, a haunting memory of terror and heartbreak.

"To have and to hold," Mariah murmured. Tears smarted in her eyes. "I never thought I'd hold you like this. I lost you, Sol, and I thought I was dying with you. Don't ever leave me again."

He raised her hand to his lips and brushed her band of gold against his whiskered cheek. "Don't cry. I'm here, and we've got the rest of our lives together. Maybe I took my vows without realizing they'd stick, but I did, and we're together from this day forward."

"You don't regret it?" she asked softly.

"I did at first, but not since I laid eyes on you." He fingered his eyepatch and she felt a quick stab of emotion. She reached up and stroked his finger away to touch the patch. Her breath caught. She knew what she was about to do wasn't wise, but she was driven by need to take their intimacy beyond sex, and slipped her finger beneath the patch.

Sol tensed and grew still. As she caressed the wound, she ached for his loss, felt his vulnerability.

"You amaze me," he said in a rough voice. "Why did you do it?"

"I wanted to touch you where no one else would. . . ."

WHAT ARE *LOVESWEPT* ROMANCES?

They are stories of true romance and touching emotion. We believe those two very important ingredients are constants in our highly sensual and very believable stories in the *LOVESWEPT* line. Our goal is to give you, the reader, stories of consistently high quality that may sometimes make you laugh, sometimes make you cry, but are always fresh and creative and contain many delightful surprises within their pages.

Most romance fans read an enormous number of books. Those they truly love, they keep. Others may be traded with friends and soon forgotten. We hope that each *LOVESWEPT* romance will be a treasure—a "keeper." We will always try to publish

LOVE STORIES YOU'LL NEVER FORGET
BY AUTHORS YOU'LL ALWAYS REMEMBER

The Editors

Loveswept ®550

Olivia Rupprecht
I Do!

BANTAM BOOKS
NEW YORK · TORONTO · LONDON · SYDNEY · AUCKLAND

I DO!

A Bantam Book / June 1992

*If you would be interested in receiving protective vinyl
covers for your Loveswept books, please write to this address
for information:*

Loveswept
Bantam Books
P.O. Box 985
Hicksville, NY 11802

ISBN 0-553-44144-2

Published simultaneously in the United States and Canada

PRINTED IN THE UNITED STATES OF AMERICA

OPM   0 9 8 7 6 5 4 3 2 1

*To He who sees beyond black and white
and has graced this seeker
with the kaleidoscope of life.*

Prologue

"Am I . . . gonna . . . die?" Sol's vision was hazy, what with his one good eye struggling to stay open. But he could tell that the young Marine's brows were pinched together as he curtly nodded. How fitting that he looked like an angel, with his head haloed by a light shining through the curtain partition in the Middle East hospital ward.

"Anything I can do for you, Sergeant?"

"Yeah. Get Turnbull. Tell him to . . . bring my gear."

Took him awhile to dredge up the words. He figured it was those damn meat cutters shooting him up good with morphine. Fact was, he'd welcome pain over numbness, this thick sensation of tingling deadweight.

"Yes, sir. Right away, sir." A sharp salute. A click of the heels. The private turned to leave, then did a quick about-face. "Your men know what you did, and we've all got a lot respect for that. Lot of respect for you, too, sir."

Sol tried to lift a bandaged arm, but couldn't. Hell of a thing, he thought. He was two hundred pounds

of muscle spread over six feet and some odd inches—
"A tall drink of water," his mom had always called
him—and he couldn't even lift his damn arm.

As he drifted off, wavering sparks of memory
washed through his drug-induced stupor. He saw
the flash of a grenade going off in a freak accident,
the trip-hammer reaction to knock his buddies out
of the way, and his own body jerking in so many
directions he felt like a marionette cut from his
strings, then flung into a boneless heap. Feeling the
jolt . . . the fire . . . the rage that it wasn't supposed to end this way. And Mariah, Mariah so sweet
upon the paper, feeling for her now as she sifted
through his head like so much regret. . . .

Should've gotten Mariah in his arms and kissed
her hard. Wonder how she kissed, how she . . .

"Sol? Yo, Sol. It's Turns. I'm here, you no-good—"
The hoarse voice, followed by a cough, roused Sol from
his musings. "Checked on Smitty and Brack. They're
both gonna make it. Now dammit, so are you."

"We'll . . . see." One ice-blue eye slitted open.
Must be seeing things. Turns wasn't no crybaby.

"I got your stuff. Guess I know what you want."

"Picture," Sol wheezed out.

"Here she is. Damn pretty sight, ain't she?"

Turns held the snapshot of a raven-haired bomb-
shell in a string bikini close to Sol's bandaged face.
She was twenty-four, six years younger than he,
with a toothpaste-commercial smile it looked like
he'd never see.

"Letter. Read it," Sol ordered.

"Which one? You must've gotten a jillion of those
perfumed babies in the last six months."

"Send me off with a . . . hot one."

"Sure, Sol. Here, this one'll give you a jump start.
Get you back on track. Sol? Sol?"

"Still here." He blinked and stared at the picture while Turns cleared his throat, then began to read.

"My darling Sol—I've already memorized your latest letter, even though I received it just yesterday. I haunt the mailbox, and I must confess that when one doesn't arrive I feel depressed, but that leaves as soon as I go to my bedroom and fill myself up with you.

"I begin with the first letter, and it makes me laugh. How stiff (ha, ha) we were with each other in the beginning. So polite and newsy and awkward. But that soon passed. We've never met, but it's as though we've known each other all our lives. You've never touched me, yet I feel we're lovers.

"Yes, I have imagined you kissing me, touching me, as you say you dream of doing in person. Thinking of it leaves me feeling empty and longing for more than this romance through the mail and our too brief phone calls.

"Since we've shared our hopes and dreams, I think it's time I told you of my deepest fear: that you'll be disappointed when you meet me at Christmas. My picture's very flattering and I'm a little shy in person. Promise me that you won't hold that against me, that you'll remember all that we've shared and give us time to know each other even better.

"After all, it's what's on the inside that counts. And on the inside, I do love you. Please write soon. And even though it's safe where you are, take good care. I'd die without you. Sending you my heart, I am yours—Mariah."

Sol's eye remained fixed on the snapshot. Letters like that had kept him celibate for the last few months. Now he was sorry he hadn't taken his pleasure with a willing female and pretended she was Mariah.

Regret, so much regret. Who knows—they might have even gotten married, after a real courtship.

But at least he'd had those letters, thanks to Operation Dear Abby. Wished he had time to send that grande dame of advice a thank you for all the mail her readers sent to the soldiers overseas. He'd reached into the mailbag like it was a Cracker Jack box and dug around for a prize that had turned out to be Mariah.

"This sucks," he mumbled as Dear Abby drifted into the ozone and a vision of Ma and Dad filled his fuzzy head. This was gonna hurt them worse than when he'd turned his back and seen to his own selfish needs. They would've loved Mariah. Mariah, so sincere and sexy, so different from Desiree . . . Mariah, saying she loved him . . . loved him . . .

"Sol? Talk to me. Hell, curse me blue, but don't leave me now."

"Get a preacher."

"What?"

"Call . . . her. Cut through the crap . . . and get us married."

"You wanna get married? You got it. Hang on, you old SOB. If you won't die on me, I'll get you married." Turns spun around and barked at an orderly. "Got a phone near?"

"Yes, sir, Lieutenant. An extension's right here. Give me a number and I'll patch you through."

"Get me a chaplain first."

"But the Padre's on furlough."

Turns lowered his voice to a hiss. "Get me anyone. He doesn't even have to say his prayers."

"But, sir, it's not standard procedure or legal or—"

"Details can wait. Can you ad-lib some wedding vows?"

"Well, sure, but—"

"Then you're it. Call Mobile, Alabama, pronto and get Mariah Garnet on the line—here's her number on the letter. Don't say anything and let me do the explaining. Got that?"

The voices were no more than faint murmurings to Sol. His mind was whirling as images of Mariah bundled him in warmth. She'd meet his parents now, have widow's benefits that might help make up for what they'd never have. And as long as she was tied to him, maybe he'd never really die. . . .

"Preacher's here, Sol. Got your lady on the phone. She knows you're banged up and wants to get hitched. We'll keep it quick and simple. All you've got to say is 'I do' when I squeeze your hand."

"Dearly beloved," the orderly began, "we are gathered—"

"Just get on with it, would ya?" Turns growled.

"Do you take this man for your lawfully wedded husband, to have to hold, for ri— Okay, okay. Do you wanna marry him?"

"I . . . I—" A feminine voice laced with molasses and tears choked on the other end. "Yes, God yes, I do. Sol? Sol, are you there? Please, Sol. I love you. Please hang on."

"And do you, Sol Standish, take this woman for—"
Turns squeezed his hand.

"I . . . do."

"By the power vested in me, I now pronounce you husband and wife. You may now kiss—"

"Want to kiss me instead, Sol?" Turns was openly crying as he leaned down toward his best friend.

"Take a . . . dive, Turns. Mariah, tell Ma . . . I—"

"Get a doctor in here! He's dying! Someone help me—"

"Stat! Stat!" A nurse thrust the wedding party out of the way. Doctors and orderlies were fast on her heels. They rushed as one into the surgical unit, where they worked over the groom's lifeless body.

One

Mariah checked her makeup in the squeaky-clean ladies' room. She dug around for some double-strength aspirin and popped three between her heavily glossed lips. Beth, her older sister, had shown her how to cake the makeup on so she'd look five years older.

Did she look twenty-four? Hardly. And even with the birth-control pills enlarging her breasts, she didn't come close to filling out Beth's sundress. At least her parents had gone on their European summer vacation once she'd convinced them that the marriage was annulled. And bless Beth for promising to help cover the truth.

Oh, the lies. How they'd multiplied, like rabbits in heat. First, the picture, one of Beth; next, giving Beth's age instead of her own.

If only she hadn't been desperate for someone to love her just for herself, with no knowledge of the cursed gift that had dogged her her entire life. If only she hadn't fallen in love with a worldly man she'd never laid eyes on. One she'd been able to reveal her soul to on paper. One who saw only her, not the prodigy who was tested ad nauseam, whose cardiologist father had tutored and displayed her, like some prize specimen, before the medical world.

She'd meant to tell Sol; really she had. And she would—once she was sure she wouldn't lose him. Then she could safely send Turns the additional papers he needed for the marriage certificate. The blood work was no problem, but her birth certificate had had her scrambling for excuses.

Turns seemed content when she'd said that it must have gotten lost in the mail, and silly her for sending the original. What he thought about her taking so long to replace it she didn't know, but he had asked her not to mention the minor holdup to Sol, since he had enough problems to deal with. She'd readily agreed, knowing it was in both their best interests.

Anyway, she didn't need to worry about the paperwork at this stage. Not when her husband might take one look at his bride and write her off as jailbait. Birth and marriage certificates wouldn't mean squat if he dumped her on sight.

Mariah pressed her forehead against the restroom mirror as the walls closed in. *Please, Lord,* she silently prayed, *let Sol love me. Give me the chance to make this crazy thing work. I know a marriage based on lies is no way to start, but without them we wouldn't be married and I'd be stuck in med school. For once, just once, I need a life of my own, something normal and real, a kindred spirit who can simply let me be . . . me.*

"Mariah? Honey, the plane's going to be here any minute," she heard LaVerne Standish say.

Grateful that the pills had taken the edge off her headache—though they hadn't done anything for her galloping heart—Mariah summoned one of Miss Lilah's Finishing School smiles for her mother-in-law.

"Thank you, Mrs. Standish. I wanted to look my best."

"Call me Mom. And, Mariah honey, you look as lovely as they come." LaVerne tilted her head. "How old did Sol say you are?"

"Twenty-four."

"Heaven above, I wish I had some of what you must be drinking. Of course, with all that milk on the farm, you're bound to keep it up."

Mariah drew in an unsteady breath, quickly swallowed another aspirin, then followed "Mom" out the door.

As the plane taxied down the runway, Sol peered out the window with his one good eye. He had trouble recognizing the small gathering near the tarmac. He had trouble recognizing himself. He was no longer a globe-trotting lifer in the service, but he wasn't a third-generation dairy farmer ready to milk his daddy's cows. Not in a million years.

A sense of failure weighed heavily upon him. Life had twisted his goals and self-image to suit everyone but himself. He wasn't even sure if he could be a husband to his wife.

He'd find out soon enough. Tonight, honeymooning in a nearby hotel. What if she cringed when she saw his eye patch, his scars? And what if he couldn't . . . The doctors had said he was just weak, depressed, or that maybe it was the medication. Easy for them to shrug it off; it wasn't their masculinity on the line.

Dear God, he prayed, *please don't strip that away from me too.* The possibility gnawed at his gut.

Five minutes passed, then ten. And still he sat there. Damn, but he wished he wasn't married, that he didn't have to think of anyone but himself. And damn Turns for saying that was just the problem and he hoped Mariah gave him holy hell, knocked the chip that ran a mile wide from off his shoulder.

If only he hadn't signed on the dotted line while he was so doped up he couldn't remember it. If only Turns hadn't taken it on himself to secure the marriage certificate. How Turns had pulled it off, Sol wasn't sure, even though he'd sort of seen it himself during one of his stupors.

Turns had claimed the certificate was now getting shuffled around. Once a record of it was entered in the Unit Diary, the Marines would recognize the marriage—not that that would make the union any more real than it already was—and send Sol the certificate for posterity.

"Posterity," he sneered. "What a concept." Without a consummation, Mariah had grounds for an annulment, and all of Turns's help would go down the tubes. Serve him right, Sol thought cynically. He was no bargain and he knew it—just as he knew Mariah mattered to him.

She mattered enough that he didn't wish himself on her.

"Sergeant? Your family's about to rush inside if you don't show fast."

With a heavy sigh, Sol used his muscular arms to pull himself up, then took the proffered crutches. But at the top of the stairs he stopped. Ma and Dad had tears in their eyes as they shouted his name and opened their arms. Their prodigal son felt the familiar rush of guilt, followed by a mind-scrambling confusion.

Who was that with them? Surely not Mariah. This looked like a scared girl, hesitantly smiling and extending her hand in a wave. Then her fingers curled into a fist, which she pressed between her daintily rounded breasts.

Sol did a double take. He frowned and saw her lips tremble. The trembling caught at him, made him feel more a man. Her open vulnerability called to his own, though he was always careful to keep it hidden.

Unable to bear showing any sign of weakness, he pitched his crutches to the attendant and grabbed on to the rails. Maybe it was cheating, but at least he would manage the steps without feeling like a cripple. They'd said he would never walk again, and yet he had. They'd said he'd need crutches for life; he couldn't buy that either.

When he stumbled on the last step, his face flushed and a profanity escaped from his flattened lips.

"Son? Son, are you okay?" His parents rushed forward as the attendant caught him from behind.

"Fine," he bit out. The glare he shot the attendant netted him his crutches, an apology, and a quick retreat. His family wasn't so easily put off. Sol stiffly endured their help amidst hugs and kisses while he scanned the girl's pretty but too-young face for any hint of distaste or pity.

No pity. Maybe a little caution, but no distaste either. He did see, however, a quick comprehension of his curtness, a deference to his stung pride. There was a maturity in her steady gaze that he recognized from her letters. *Mariah.* His wife wasn't what he'd expected. She was less. And in some unfathomable way, she was more.

Without warning, he felt a flicker of desire. He was as grateful for that as for her silent understanding. She didn't threaten his masculinity; indeed, she reassured him of it, even as she took a timid step forward.

She was a little slip of a woman, he realized with shock. Either the picture had lied or she'd lost a good twenty pounds since she'd sent it. Of course, he'd put her through hell, nearly dying on her like that, and emotional turmoil had a way of taking a physical toll, as he knew.

"Excuse me, Ma and Dad. If you don't mind, I'd like to meet my wife."

With a final hug and a slap on the back, his parents broke away, giving him room to maneuver his crutches. Damn, how he hated these things. He hobbled ten feet that seemed like a mile, until he stood head and shoulders over his bride.

The earlier flicker intensified, stirring him close to arousal as she stared up at him with wide brown eyes. He thought they would be light, maybe gray, judging from her picture. But he was glad they weren't, feeling himself drawn deeply into their depths. Sweet as chocolate, as elusive as a skittish doe's blinded by light.

"Mariah?"

"Sol? Is it really you?"

"I was thinking the same about you."

She toyed with a runaway curl from her upswept hair. It had the vibrant richness he recognized, only more of a reddish mahogany. Maybe she'd colored it.

Whatever the discrepancies, he didn't much care at the moment. She was causing some definite physical reactions in him, reactions he clung to and that gave him the reassurance he desperately needed: He *was* still a man.

"Welcome home." Struggling to appear calm, she offered her hand. Did a handshake strike him as absurd, too? she wondered. The awkward moment passed at first touch. A sense of connection washed over her, followed by a definite tingle that began in her fingertips and spread up her arms when he pressed a soft kiss on her palm.

"You make me feel welcome." His voice was deep, rich, and had no small effect on her unsteady nerves. "And a little more ready to accept coming home."

His brief remarks eased her somewhat. She could feel herself smiling, even as her heart took a dive. Despite his smart full-dress uniform, he was a ghost of his photograph, though he still gave her the sensation of gazing at a chart-topping heartthrob.

The planes of his face were finely crafted, but too sharp for him to be remotely pretty. It was a face that bespoke hard-earned maturity. A strong chin, with a shadow of a beard; ice-blue eye; short, gold-tipped hair; full lips that had been terribly stern when he'd frowned but were achingly sensual as they softened and returned her hopeful smile—all blended together to strangely affect her vital signs.

Pulse: too rapid. Breathing: irregular. Internal temperature: simultaneously dropping and feverishly high. Diagnosis: The man she was in love with turned her on. A man who was still fairly whole, if she didn't count the eye patch, the drag of a bad leg, or Turns's warning about some deeper wounding that wasn't physical.

As he stood looming over her, his shadow dwarfing her slight frame, she remembered her father saying how patients should never be treated as invalids if they were to heal.

"You sure picked a pretty one, son," Dad said with hearty approval.

"And such a lady, too," Ma chimed in.

"Yes," Sol murmured, as he fingered his eye patch and studied her too incisively. The piercing brightness of his one good eye pinned her where she stood and quickened her pulse to a hot-ice rush.

She felt as if he were looking all the way through her and seeing each damning lie. Mariah could almost feel herself shrinking, while Sol seemed to grow in stature. He was so big, the aura he projected so formidable. He wore his years with ease, making her lack of them excruciatingly real.

While the trio continued to discuss her with open interest, she suddenly felt like crying out that she was a fraud. With great effort, she pasted on a schooled smile and made the polite responses.

"Think maybe you could pick up my bags and bring the car around?" Sol suggested to his folks, then took a step closer to Mariah. Her heart was pounding so hard with anticipation and dread, she wondered if he could hear it rattle against her ribs.

LaVerne looked from one to the other and Mariah caught her knowing smile before she nudged Herbert away.

"You'll have to excuse us old folks, Mariah. We've been married so long we forgot you kids are on your honeymoon. Why, Sol hasn't even gotten to kiss his bride."

Mariah's cheeks grew warm; Sol quirked a brow. Unexpectedly, he smiled broadly. His teeth were even and pearly white, gleaming as if they belonged to a wolf and he was contemplating taking more than a bite.

The ground seemed to shift, leaving her wobbly on her feet. She wished for a loan of his crutches.

"They're gone, Mariah. Now it's just you and me."
His grin faded. Mariah swallowed hard and hugged
her waist. "We have to talk, because there are some
things that need to be said before we head for the
hotel. The answers I get will make a difference as to
whether or not we go."

"You're disappointed," she blurted before she
could stop herself. "I know you expected me to be
prettier and . . . and—"

She glanced down at the front of her sundress,
blinking against the quick sting behind her eyes.
Mariah expected him to say he'd found her out; she
expected him to confront and kindly chide her, and
then to demand an immediate annulment.

What she didn't expect was the feel of his fingertip
tipping up her chin, or his thumb stroking her
bottom lip.

"Disappointed?" he said in a low voice. "Hardly.
Just a little surprised. I feel like an old man next to
you, like I've been put out to pasture while you
should be running free for greener grass. It's only
right for me to turn you loose. Bolt if you want to."

"I'm your wife, Sol. I meant my vows when I took
them. Don't think for a minute that I want to take
them back."

His thumb moved with each word she spoke,
creating a friction that stole her breath. Or maybe it
was fear that he was only being kind, offering her a
way to save face.

Sol drew back his thumb and fingered his black
eye patch self-consciously. "When you said 'I do,'
this wasn't part of the bargain."

Mariah wasn't aware of her action until she'd
actually gripped his wrist. It put her hand close to
his eye patch. The strip that held it in place slashed

his dark, frowning brow and looped behind his white dress cap.

Sol was too still; she wanted to move from his pinpoint glare, but fought the urge. The moment was too crucial for her to back down.

"I think that patch bothers you, Sol, a lot more than it does me."

"I don't doubt it, because it bothers me a helluva lot." He gazed hatefully at his crutches. "They say I'll never walk without these."

"Do you believe it?"

"I don't want to."

"But do you believe it?"

"No."

"Then neither do I." Somehow, she found the courage to find out exactly where she stood with him. "If you want out because you married me with the idea we'd never meet, or if I'm less than what you'd hoped for—"

"I didn't say that!"

"No, but that doesn't mean you didn't think it. If that's the reason you're trying to run me off, why you'd rather spend your time glaring at me instead of . . . of kissing me, then fine. We both know you bought into this marriage without either of us certain what we were going to end up with, and, and—" Her voice caught on a sharp emotional chord, her doubts rolling out before she could stop them.

"Mariah, please, don't do this."

"No, *you* please be quiet and just listen to me." She couldn't believe her own words, but she was glad to have them said and done with. "If you want out, consider yourself out. But if you expect me to jump ship because your body's taken some abuse, then you've got a lot to learn about the woman you took as wife, Mr. Standish."

Two

He stared at her hard, but she refused to flinch. Slowly, his lips softened and quirked up at one end, lips that were generous and demanded her undivided attention.

"It appears, Mrs. Standish, that I underestimated you." Her grip still on his wrist, he shifted his hand to touch his thumb to her lip once more. Her eyes nearly closed. He was so near she could feel his breath on her. "Where would you suggest that I begin my education?"

"A wedding kiss?" she whispered.

"Why don't we start with one for hello and work our way from there." His lips met hers for the first time, a feather-soft brush that teased and tempted, a tantalizing sample that made her press closer and resent his stinginess.

"Hello, Mariah."

"How do you do, Sol?"

"Thanks to you, better than I can remember for quite some time. But not nearly as good as I'd feel if that lipstick was as much on my mouth as it is on yours."

It was just about the sexiest thing a man had ever said to her. And Sol was most definitely a man, she realized with an alarming thrill as he pressed against her belly. She hesitantly slipped her arms around his waist to urge him nearer.

"You affect me," he said with a rush of relief she didn't know how to take. "Thank God, you do. But the way I look now, I wonder if I can do the same for you."

Mariah nervously wet her lips. What should she say? That her knees were knocking, her stomach was bottoming out, and this worldly man, who seemed to need some kind of reassurance from her, was causing an exquisite aching between her unsteady legs?

"You feel good to me," she said uncertainly, then hazarded a quick kiss to buy the moment's time she was in desperate need of.

"Good's . . . not bad." He sounded disappointed.

"More than good," she said quickly, then plunged heedlessly forward. "You excite me."

"Do I?" His tone was cautious. "Does that mean you feel a little twinge? Or can I hope for more, that maybe you're actually looking forward to tonight?"

"Are you?"

"I'm eager. And a little apprehensive."

"Me too." She traced the line of his mouth with her fingers, wondering if he could feel them shaking. "That's always the way it was with our letters, Sol. Feeling the same way about the same things." Except that she'd declared her love and he hadn't. But he had married her, and that surely counted for something.

"It's different in person. But I'm glad to say it's not awkward. You're comfortable to be with, Mariah, and a little comfort's something I could use." He moved slightly against her, and something liquid and hot slid through her insides. "It's been a long time since I was intimate with a woman."

How curious this seemed, she thought, to have just met and be so open. But more curious was that she didn't feel embarrassed by his frankness. It prompted her to try saying what she would have on paper.

"And I've never been . . . well, I've never been unfaithful to you, Sol."

"That pleases me. Greatly. I just hope that I can please you later, that I haven't lost my touch." His brow furrowed as he appeared to debate with himself. Then, with a determined expression, he discreetly pressed a palm to her breast.

Instant heat generated a spine-tingling chill. Air caught in her lungs, then rushed out on a startled gasp.

"I know it's not the time or place, and I can't explain it to you, but there's something I can't wait to assure myself about." His hand was hidden between their chests like an illicit secret, and he fondled her with the proprietary claim of a husband. "Do you mind?"

"Dear God," she moaned. She'd never heard herself make such a deep, catching sound before.

"Answer enough. Now kiss your husband, Mrs. Standish. Make it hard and deep. Show me you really mean it."

Mariah's head fell back, her neck arched, and her lips parted. Sol's low chuckle made her eyes open wide, and she felt a quick stab of fear that in her newfound passion she was amusing.

"Uh-uh, babe. I want you to kiss *me*."

He wanted a kiss? One that was hard and deep? Well, by golly, she was going to give him one, one that would make up for every lie she'd concocted to be with him now.

For all her bravado, Mariah's hand trembled as she threaded her fingers into his sand-colored hair and urged his head down. His hat fell to the ground as she slanted her mouth against his. Smooth . . . flexible . . . generous to a fault.

She nibbled at the pliable lobes, delighting in the low sound he made, exulting in the sense that this was so right, it felt almost sinful.

Sin had never tasted so fine. It tasted fine enough to mute the shame of her dishonesty. She squelched what remained of it with the dart of her tongue. His teeth were slick and as hard as the thickening arousal she felt through their clothes.

How many times had she dreamed of this?

His shoulders against her palms suddenly tensed and she felt them shift with his unexpected retreat.

Automatically, she went on tiptoe to follow his mouth.

"Damn," he groaned. "Damn, but I needed that from you. Now it's my turn to return the favor." He dropped one crutch to the ground, balanced himself with a strength that struck her as oddly graceful for such a powerfully built man, and flattened his palm against her spine, fingers fanning out, then flexing into her upper buttocks. "Open your mouth," he whispered roughly.

She did, with a soft squeak, shockingly excited by the overt sexuality of his handling, not to mention his blunt demand. He was speaking to her as a woman, putting his hand on her as he if she were truly his wife and he had every right to touch her however he liked.

His lips covered hers and his tongue quickly entered her mouth. She embraced him with equal passion, like a woman full grown. The sensuality between them was heavy, binding them, entwining their future paths.

Sol didn't kiss her with any hint of restraint. Nor did she return it with the awkwardness of a mail-order bride.

Their kiss was wet. It was hot. His tongue was impolite and so were his teeth. She felt their pull on her bottom lip and the rhythmic squeeze of his hand on her breast. Sensations arced and centered to tug at her womb. The strain of his pants was anchored there, and while he didn't behave indecently, he bumped against her once, then pressed hard. It was wildly exciting to her, like a forbidden pleasure they indulged to the limits, skirting the edge as close as they could without falling off the precipice.

"Yes," he was mouthing against her. "Yes, it's so good." And then he murmured something else, something that sounded like a thank you, though she couldn't imagine why he should thank her when he was the one imparting this magic heat.

As Sol grazed a path from her swollen lips to her chin, she decided her husband had elevated the act of kissing to an art. Especially when he briefly drew her chin into the haven of his mouth before leaving it moist and pulsing against the assault of emotion-charged air.

His breathing was harsh, but surely no harsher than hers, which she could barely catch in choppy spurts. The heat of his gaze mingled with something else. He looked as if he'd just won first prize and she was it.

"My goodness," she finally said, unsure of what to do after such a torrid encounter. "That was . . . quite a kiss."

"You approve?"

"Well, yes. I do." *I do . . . I do . . .* Their hasty vows echoed between her ears, and the reality of it hit her strongly. Married. To this man. One who was flesh and blood, not paper or a phone call, who touched with emotion and kissed like the devil. What would he be like to live with? If he had a temper to match his kisses, she sure didn't want to provoke it.

"I approve too," he said quietly. "Of you." Sol fingered his patch. It gleamed at her like a demon in the dark as his lips drew into a tight, thin line. "In fact, I approve so much I'm giving you one last chance, because you deserve it. You can leave with a kiss and I won't blame you. But go with me now and there's no turning back."

She held his gaze in silence, then gave him her answer by stooping down to pick up his hat and crutch. She held out the latter to him. "You'll need this to get to the car."

"I could've gotten it myself," he said sharply.

Mariah was stung, but she did understand.

"In that case . . ." Putting his pride before her own, she laid the crutch back down. "Get it your-self."

Sol seemed off balance, in more than a physical way. He frowned at her hard, then nodded curtly.

"Thanks, I will." He started to bend down, but stopped short. "You go on. I'll catch up."

"I'd rather we go together, and I don't mind the wait."

His curse was low but graphic, the sort of word she imagined might be scratched out next to a toilet in a seedy bar. She heard a few more that weren't any nicer as he awkwardly stooped and contorted him-self to get both crutches in place.

Sol was sweating by the time he propelled himself forward, his gaze straight ahead. He was a good twenty feet away from her when she turned on Beth's best high-heels and marched after him. As she came closer she grappled with more unknowns than their impending honeymoon. His scars ran deeper than his obvious injuries, she was certain. She also knew healing was slow, but she'd bought time.

When she came even with him, Sol slowed his fast-paced swing.

"Thanks," he said tersely.

"For what? Letting you make your point?"

"For understanding. Letting me stand on my own two feet, such as they are." He speeded up, then pivoted, blocking her path. "I'm sorry I snapped at you, Mariah. It's not your fault I'm mad at God and the world."

"No," she said. "But it is your fault if you let your anger steal the joy you can still have from life."

For a while he considered her and, she hoped, what she'd said. When he spoke, his tone was apologetic, but she didn't think it came easy.

"You gave me some real joy back there. I didn't pay you back very kindly."

"Then pay me back later by not taking my help as pity. You don't want it and I don't have it to give to a man I respect. Oh, and while you're paying up, do me a favor and don't try offering me my walking papers again."

Maybe it was the sudden brightness in his eye. Maybe it was the gentling of his lips into a slight smile. Whatever it was, she followed her heart and impulsively bent down to kiss his wedding band, gleaming against the crutch.

She felt, rather than saw, his right hand release its hold on the wood to lay against her head.

"You're beautiful, you know that?"

Mariah beamed. Beautiful? That was always reserved for Beth. "Pleasantly pretty" had always been
the compliment she received. Unless she counted
"brilliant" or "beyond her years" or "model child"—
though the last one she'd ditched for good.

Sol retrieved his hat from her grasp and to her
amazement perched it on top of her upswept hair. He
winked.

"Pretty as a picture," he pronounced. "And speaking of pictures, I've been thinking about the one you
sent me."

"Yes?" she croaked, the nasty taste of guilt lodging
in her throat. "What about my picture?"

"It was something to drool over, all right." His
warm, sexy smile turned the asphalt under her feet
to sinking sand. "But, Mariah, it didn't do you
justice."

Three

Mariah felt Sol's arm tighten around her shoulders once they were settled in the backseat of his parents' shiny new Lincoln. How good his touch felt, how perfectly right; and yet, it held an undeniable tension that hummed of anticipation and unknowns. A contradiction, she realized, just as Sol and his parents were contradictions.

Unlike their son, Herbert and LaVerne Standish didn't seem complex. They were plain people, putting on no airs, but exuding a quite dignity. Just as their clothes were understated but of obvious quality. Mariah recognized money when she saw it and they had more than enough to get by, though they'd said many dairy farmers were struggling. Hard workers both, according to Sol. His parents were always up before the crack of dawn to see to the running of their eight-hundred-acre farm, where two hundred cows produced over twenty thousand quarts of milk a day.

"You're quiet back there, Mariah." LaVerne leaned around and smiled. "Being a parent, I can't help but wonder what your folks think of all this. A boy's one thing, but a girl's another when it comes to being protective. Aren't they just a little concerned, since they haven't met their son-in-law? Sol's a fine man, but they can't know that themselves."

Mariah stiffened, then quickly relaxed before Sol could interpret her reaction for what it was.

"Well, they're curious, of course. But they trust my judgment, and knowing how much Sol means to me, they wished us every happiness."

"How nice, giving their blessing sight unseen. I suppose they'll want to meet him soon, though. In fact, I half expected them to fly up here with you, to see your new home." LaVerne nodded with obvious pride at her son. "And husband."

"No, not yet!" When Sol abruptly stopped stroking Mariah's arm, she hastily added, "I mean, they're in Europe this summer."

"Oh?" Sol said with interest. "As soon as they get back they'll have to come for a visit. But if you're feeling a little homesick, we can always go there. I'm eager to meet them too."

Stifling a groan, Mariah thanked heaven for Miss Lilah's training and primly folded her hands in her lap to disguise their shaking.

"Yes, we'll have something to look forward to." Lair, liar, pants on fire, her conscience taunted. "Perhaps by fall we'll be settled and everyone can get together then."

"Great." Sol reached for her hand and rubbed his thumb over the sweaty palm. "Just so they come before the snow starts to fly. I never thought to ask, but have you ever experienced a northern winter?"

"Not yet." And if she didn't figure a way out of this predicament she'd made, she might never. "How cold is it?"

"Lots of babies born from midsummer to early fall, if that tells you anything," Herbert answered, chuckling. "It's so darn cold outside sometimes it hurts to breathe. No wonder Wisconsin's the brandy-consumption capital of the world. Warms a body up almost as good as other things. Right, Vernie?" He winked at his wife.

"Herbert!" LaVerne swatted at him, but laughed. "What's Mariah to think of us with you talking like that?"

That you're a lot more fun-loving and down-to-earth than my mom and dad, she thought. Not that her parents weren't good in their hearts, but she did find the difference refreshing. She liked the Standishes. They had accepted her without question, made her feel a part of something wholesome that was meat-and-potatoes real.

"From Appleton to Yuba, there's a Friday fish fry in every restaurant and corner tavern with a kitchen stove." Sol's tone was flat. "Green Bay Packers and beer are serious careers. Cheese-and-milk is the state religion."

"Fortunately for us," his mother put in, shooting Sol a sharp glance.

Mariah sensed an unaccountable stress filling the silence as Sol turned his attention out the window to the passing blur of green hills and lush, towering trees.

"I'm sure it's beautiful in the winter," she said, hoping to ease the tension. "Everything covered in white."

"Just like a Currier and Ives painting," LaVerne said, though her attention remained on Sol's remote profile. "You should see the kids sledding, having a ball. Even Sol liked that when he was young. You remember that, son?"

"Yeah, I remember." His sigh was heavy. Mariah saw the flash of hurt in his mother's eyes before Sol turned and forced a slight smile. "The sleigh rides were always a good time too, Ma. Maybe we can hitch up the horses and take Mariah for a spin before Christmas. Would you like that?"

"A real sleigh ride?" she exclaimed.

"Complete with jingle bells on the horses." When she smiled, a dazzling smile of pure excitement, his troubled gaze warmed. "We'll bundle up good together in the back and share a flask of brandy."

"I'd love it! I've never seen snow, except for the little flurry Mobile had once when I was in the fourth grade. All the schools were even let out."

"That reminds me, Mariah, didn't Sol say you've got a degree in biology, that you left a job in a hospital lab to move up here?"

The excitement drained from her, along with the color in her face. She nodded, managing a wooden smile.

"I'll bet they hated to lose you," LaVerne commented.

"Not really. I didn't work there quite a year." Never, actually, she thought bitterly, unless you count watching my dad perform open-heart surgery or being a game of scientific Trivial Pursuit for his cronies. Or memorizing the medical library in my spare time.

"A year?" Sol's brow furrowed. "For some reason I thought it was longer. Didn't you get your degree two years ago?"

"Well, I—yes." At least, she could have, she told herself. Only she'd dragged her feet to keep from graduating from college before her own age group got their high school diplomas. Not that it changed anything. She was still the oddball, a freak. Too mentally advanced for her chronological peers; too young to be more than a curiosity to her intellectual peers.

"What did you do in your off time? I wouldn't think you'd be hard pressed to find a job in your field."

Desperate for a credible explanation, she latched on to some more of Beth's history. "I traveled. Through Europe and the Orient."

"And here I thought I knew most everything there was to know about you." Sol's gaze was wistful. "We've got more in common than I realized. I love to travel."

"Don't we know it," LaVerne muttered. Herbert nodded.

"What was your favorite country in Europe?" His grip tightening on her hand, Sol looked at her as if she were as much a newfound best friend as a wife. "France? Italy?"

"Spain." Mariah's stomach bottomed out when she caught herself about to say the Swiss Alps; she'd already claimed she'd never seen more than a snow flurry. "The people were nice and the food was wonderful. But I liked the scenery best of all."

"Me too. And what about the Orient? Did you have a favorite spot there?"

"Thailand." Oh Lord, what had Beth said about that place, the one that was so exotic? Bangkok, that was it. She even remembered a few of the places Beth had said she'd visited. "Bangkok was a lot of fun. So much to see and do."

"I'll say," Sol agreed. "Did you try any of their better restaurants?"

"Mostly out-of-the-way places. But I remember, um, having curried squid at—Swahilli's."

"Excellent place, Swahilli's. Just think, Mariah,

our paths could have crossed and we didn't even know it."

"That's something to imagine, isn't it?"

"Where else did you go? Anywhere for entertainment?"

She was so queasy, Mariah considered pleading car sickness to stop this horrible conversation. If she could just get to a library and memorize a few travel books. . . .

"There was a place called . . . Pat Pong's?"

Sol stared at her blankly. Then he cleared his throat and said, "I'm not sure I heard right. Did you just say Pat Pong's?"

"Uh-huh."

He leaned closer and seemed to study her in a new light. "And what did you think about the, er, entertainment?"

"It was . . . nice."

"Nice?" He appeared to be strangling on a laugh. He was also moving his palm from her knee to under her dress, then squeezing the inside of her leg.

"Well, maybe *nice* isn't the word. Interesting."

"Umm . . . yes. And did you, by chance, find it . . . exciting?"

"Oh yes, extremely exciting."

Sol's brow lifted; his gaze heated up several degrees, and his hand moved higher.

"Why don't we pick up this conversation in more private surroundings?" he whispered intimately. Then he darted the tip of his tongue into her ear before nipping a lobe and drawing away.

"Uh . . . sure." She had no idea what she'd said to arouse him, but Sol was looking at her as if he were a tom on the prowl and she a cat in heat. Mariah mentally crossed herself and prayed for some divine intervention.

"Of course, we don't have to talk," he murmured. "I'd just as soon enact some of Pat Pong's entertainment. That is, if you're in agreement with me on what their most exciting show is."

"I—what's your favorite?" she whispered back.

"Given the variety of erotic acts they show on stage, that's a tough decision. But the one that comes most to mind was the man and woman who choreographed the most amazing ways to make love."

"Mariah? The champagne's getting warm." Sol checked his watch. "I know you're probably nervous, babe, but this is ridiculous. You've been in that bathroom forever."

"I'll—I'll be out in a minute."

"I'll give you five, but that's it."

Shaking his head, Sol made his way to the champagne bottle and uncorked it. He'd wanted to open it with Mariah in a joint celebration, but the pain was getting bad and he wasn't taking the chance of pills numbing his body.

Since he was alone, he didn't bother with a glass. Drinking several gulps, he was relieved to feel an easing of the needlelike stabs running through his left leg.

He'd taken his shirt off but left his pants on, afraid the sight would turn Mariah cold. Maybe it was vanity; maybe it was that she'd been skittish as a newborn calf since they'd arrived in their honeymoon suite. First, she'd been hungry but didn't want room service. He'd taken her downstairs and fed her, but she'd barely touched her food. She did drink two glasses of wine, however.

It had struck him as odd that she claimed to have

lost her ID when the waiter carded her. His own assurance that she was of age brought the wine with no further problems, but she acted even more off balance than she had in the car.

Sol took another long swig, then poured two glasses. Yeah, she was on edge all right, jumpy. Her poise at the base had seemed to fade with each mile that brought them closer to the hotel. Wedding-night jitters? After all, she'd never met her groom before today. Or was it more?

Sol went to the mirror and studied his reflection. He was no longer what people back home had called movie-star handsome, not with the patch and several thin crisscross scars etching his face and neck. Looks had never been too important to him—until they'd been taken away. Maybe he should have accepted that glass eye he'd been offered instead of deciding Mariah would take him as is or not at all.

Snarling at his image, he stared at his bare chest. It was marred by the big, ugly red scar riding the middle of his breastbone—the result of having his chest opened and his heart massaged back into beating.

No, he wasn't a pretty sight. He could almost wish that they had let him die.

But Mariah had made him glad to be alive today. She'd hit home with her words about letting anger steal his joy. Only looking at himself now, he didn't see much to be happy about, and he sure as hell wasn't thrilled with her sudden lack of responsiveness. He didn't know what had cooled her off, but he was going to find out.

Unsightly or not, he wanted her. *Needed* her, more than he'd ever needed anyone before. He needed her companionship, the sound of her sweet, sexy, molasses drawl, the support she offered.

And right now, he needed her in bed. Maybe he could lose his pain inside her.

Abruptly turning from the mirror, Sol went over to the bathroom door. He rapped, then jiggled the knob.

Locked.

"Time's up, Mariah," he said with the authority he used on his men. "Come out of there and I mean *now.*"

He thought he heard a muffled sob over the sound of running water. *Lord, was the idea of laying with him that horrible?* All his self-doubts rose up with a vengeance. But then he clenched his jaw and his hand drew into a fist, as determination—the same grit that had made liars of the doctors who said he'd never walk—drew him up as taut as a bowstring.

He was going to give his wife a night of passion that would make Pat Pong's shows seem tame. By the time he was through, she wouldn't care what the hell he looked like under the sheets. But first he had to coax her out.

Holding down his impatience, Sol gentled his tone.

"Please, Mariah . . . honey . . . I wish you'd open the door. I won't attack you, I promise. We'll just sit and talk for a while, sip our champagne. If you want to, we can even turn on the TV and try to find an old movie"—*like hell*—"and order up some popcorn, just like we said in our letters. Come on now, open the door."

Four

"Be right there, Sol." Mariah quickly patted her tear-streaked face dry with the towel she'd cried in. Oh, that terrible ride in the car, then the ID. And Sol thinking she'd actually gone to a sordid place and was excited by it!

She hastily threw on some lipstick and mascara, then ran some concealer over her puffy red nose. Realizing she had big pink splotches on her chest, she rubbed some concealer over those also. The deep V of her white negligee plunged low between her fingertips. Beth had helped her pick out the revealing lingerie—had, in fact, loved every minute of the intrigue. The "perfect little daughter" had finally fallen from grace, with a thump, and the elder black sheep had delighted in having some company.

Mariah pulled a brush through her shoulder-length hair, took several deep breaths, and slowly opened the door.

The smile she'd pasted on disappeared as she came to eye level with a massive dark chest bearing a telltale scar of trauma. Lord, he hadn't told her that they had cracked his chest. Brutal as the emergency entry had been to get to his heart, the stitch work had been beautifully executed.

But that wasn't what made her own solar plexis feel a sweet impaling. It was the reality of this man in his prime. A man crafted of tough muscle, abused but somehow harshly majestic for it, full of character and masculine strength.

She was so mesmerized by the sight, she couldn't stop her gaze from searching for more. The diamond pattern of chest hair disappeared beneath the waistband of low-riding pants. The belt was undone, a gold buckle angling beside his fly.

Mariah reached for the door frame to steady herself, but Sol caught her hand instead. When he laid it against his chest, she felt the jolt of the contact so fiercely he could have been sliding his hand between her legs.

"I missed you," he said in a thick voice. "But what I'm seeing now more than makes up for the wait."

Mariah searched for her voice and something to say. After several moments, she murmured, "My sister, Beth, helped me pick it out. Usually I wear an oversize T-shirt to bed. I'm afraid this is a little risqué for me."

"Not for me."

She felt the escalation of his heartbeat beneath her palm and lifted her gaze. The trek from his awesome chest to neck, strong jaw, and sensual mouth took a long time.

And then time stopped completely as his eye snared hers. His look was that of a man whose purpose was firm, and that purpose was the bodily possession of his wife. A hot sensation filled, then gushed down from, her belly.

Sol's attention drifted down to her flimsily clad breasts. Though he'd caressed her there before, she felt a rush of modesty. His gaze was undressing her, arousing sensations that were frightening in their intensity. What was happening wasn't as safe as reading a steamy letter, or watching a love scene in a movie. *A movie!*

"You—you said something about finding an old movie and ordering up some popcorn?"

"All I'm interested in now is getting my hands on your skin." He slipped a hand beneath white silk and weighed her breast in his palm. When she jumped, he murmured soothingly, "Relax, relax. I just need to touch you, that's all."

His ease only heightened her lack of it. And her confusion grew as his warm, large fingers became suddenly busy with slowly, gently kneading her soft flesh. Mariah was drowning in a pool of feelings she didn't know what to do with. When Sol thumbed a nipple, Mariah thought she would die.

Then he uncovered her breasts. He stared at her nakedness, doing nothing to disguise the fact that he liked what he saw.

"I agree with you that Pat Pong's was exciting," he said, "but not half as arousing as touching, looking at, or, as I'm going out of my mind wanting to find out, tasting your breasts."

With no more warning than that, he bent and flicked his tongue over a single nipple.

Mariah staggered back against the bathroom door. For one moment she considered running back in there and staying long enough to escape from this physical, emotional wilderness, and to emerge with some sense of balance.

She couldn't form a coherent thought, couldn't react with the response he seemed to expect. The best she could do was to grasp his shoulders and push him away.

"I—I want to—to watch a movie," she stuttered. "Call for the popcorn. I need some champagne."

Mariah rushed past him, her eyes glued to the filled glass. Thank goodness she didn't have to pour it; she'd surely slosh it all over the carpet.

When she frantically brought the glass to her lips, he caught her gaze. And she saw that the blatant lust that had simmered in his eye had turned hard.

"You want to watch movies on our honeymoon night? Fine," he gritted out. "Catch me up on the action when I get back. I'm headed for the bar."

With amazing speed, Sol went to the closet and got his shirt and dress coat. He was unzipping his pants to tuck the shirttail in by the time she realized he was actually going to leave. Mariah caught a flash of white briefs. The large hands that minutes ago had been skillfully fondling her breasts were now holding crutches.

"Sol. Wait! Please, wait. Don't leave."

"Too late. I'm gone," he threw over his shoulder as she rushed to stop him.

"I'm sorry. God, I'm so sorry. I didn't mean to hurt your feelings."

"I can't afford feelings right now—not with a smashed-up leg that's smarting like hell. Don't wait up. I'll be back when I can deal with a wife who finds me so revolting she doesn't want me to touch her."

"No! No, it's not that way at all." She reached him as his hand grasped the knob. "Don't go. Stay. Forget the movie. I'm just nervous, that's all. It's not your fault, it's mine."

"Right," he snapped, still facing the door. "It's not your fault I'm so disfigured you can't stand to have me put my hands on you, or look at you without two eyes. I can't blame you. I doubt that *I'd* want to go to bed with me."

"That's not true! I do—"

"Oh yeah? Could've fooled me. Admit it, Mariah, you don't want to get pawed by someone who's less than a whole man. If that's how you feel, it's no skin off my teeth." He twisted the knob. "You probably don't want *those* on your perfect body, either."

Mariah caught his wrist, stunned by the anger in his tone, anger that was directed not only at her, but at himself.

"Don't be ridiculous. This has nothing to do with your injuries."

"No? As far as I can see you're nothing but a liar, and that's one trait I can't abide." She flinched. "Go on, Mariah, go watch your movie. I'd rather get drunk than take a wife to bed who's sleeping with me out of duty."

"Duty? I never said, never thought—How can you believe I'd even think such a thing?"

"I didn't, until you ran for the booze and begged for a movie instead of me. I just hope to God the rest of our marriage isn't as disappointing as tonight. Somehow I didn't plan on some serious drinking and thinking about a woman who shudders every time I show my heart or the rest of my body—even if they *are* both imperfect."

"How dare you imply that I'm so shallow and insensitive that I would shun anyone—much less you—who's been hurt? I resent that as much as those ugly words you've tried to put in my mouth. And all because I showed some modesty when you—"

"Touched my wife, who admitted to getting off on watching strangers have sex on a stage. But apparently that doesn't extend to me." Sol looked away from her. "I've lost too much, Mariah. My pride's about the only thing left, and it's not yours for the taking. I'm keeping it. Just as you can keep your pity screw."

Mariah clamped one hand on his arm and covered his grip on the knob with the other. She tugged and pulled but he was immovable. He was shutting her out, putting distance between them so he could cling to his hurt, his bitterness. With nothing to lose but her heart, she honed in on Sol's most vulnerable spot.

"So you want to keep your pride," she said sharply. "That's no problem, since I can't take anything you're not willing to give up. But as for pity, you don't need mine. You're wallowing in enough of your own. Go on, Sol, leave, take the easy way out. I gathered from our ride that you've been running away from some things. You might as well add me to the list."

Sol's spine stiffened. She could all but see his hair bristle on end and knew that she had achieved her purpose—perhaps too well. He swiveled around with go-to-hell rage.

Only his legs didn't catch up with the rage. Sluggish, they twisted behind his torso, and he stumbled trying to gain his footing. Mariah caught him by the shoulders, but his weight was twice hers and they both fell to the floor.

Crutches landed with a soft thump on either side of her head. The breath was knocked from her lungs—or maybe it was the solid weight of Sol's chest pinning hers down. Or the sudden awareness that his hipbones were riding over hers while his groin was pressing between the hollow of her wide-open legs.

The air he sucked in and out between groans

fanned her ear, and his lightly whiskered cheek scratched her temple. She felt an unexpected thickening rise and lodge between her thighs.

"Are you all right?" he said raggedly. "Did I hurt you?"

"I'm . . . fine. But what about you, your leg? Is it hurting?"

"I'm hurting, in more places than I can juggle at the moment. Give me a minute and I'll get off."

Mariah realized that her hips were arching for a closer fit. Sol groaned and started to roll to the side, but she automatically gripped his shoulders to stop him. She wasn't sure why she'd done it, except that she was caught in a tingling pleasure that he'd take with him if he left. No, she didn't want him to move. And she sure as heck didn't want him to go out that door. Acting on instinct, she brazenly wrapped a leg around one of his.

Sol looked down at her with a questioning gaze. She met it with one of her own. He had the answers; she needed to discover them.

"Mariah," he said in a strained voice, "I think you'd best let me go. I might be in bad shape, but I'm still a man."

"I know." She traced his lips with a shaking fingertip. "I never thought otherwise, Sol, only you wouldn't listen."

"Then why did you bolt?"

For once she found the courage to give him the truth. "Because you *are* a man. More of a man than I've ever had occasion to deal with."

The lift of his brow expressed his disbelief, but he didn't argue. Instead he firmly removed her hands from his shoulders and raised them high above her head, causing her breasts to draw up and separate. And then she felt his thumbnail flick over her nipples until they were distended and acute with a pleasurable pain.

As soon as she moaned, he placed his hands on either side of her head and moved between her spread legs. He pushed against her, rotated, withdrew, then repeated the movement. She felt him grow harder, and she more aroused.

His face intense, he ended the breath-stealing thrusts with a grind that left her feeling achingly hollow inside.

"It just so happens that I believe words are cheap," he rasped. "Now let's see if yours are more truth than lie."

With that, he maneuvered the silk gown between them to her waist, breached the thin barrier of panties, and felt the truth for himself.

The most acute sensation speared her and emerged as a loud moan from her throat.

His eye glistened with heated pleasure while his fingertips continued to gently explore.

"You want me," he said with unmistakable relief. "Scars and all, if bodies don't lie."

She wasn't sure what she wanted; she only knew that it began with a letter, an innocent fib, and culminated in this ecstasy that was tearing her apart.

"I'm sorry I lashed out at you," she whispered haltingly. "But I couldn't let you leave."

A single finger, then two, pushed inside her, and his thumb found her sensitive point.

"I'm glad you didn't. I was wrong." His teeth caught at her chin before he drew it into his mouth. "But so were you," he said, now shifting to dart a tongue through her lips. "Right or wrong, I was raised to believe a wife shouldn't speak with such disrespect to her husband."

"And I was raised to—" He stopped her words by taking her hand and pressing her fingers over the significant bulge in his pants. Then he led them to his zipper. With a shuddering intake of breath, she pulled the zipper down while expressing her last coherent thought. "I was raised to believe that a man doesn't provoke his wife to . . . to be disrespectful, by showing respect for her. You hurt me, Sol. I bit back."

"Bite me now. Here, on my shoulder, my mouth. If you draw blood, it can't be any more painful than thinking you didn't want me for better or worse. Kiss me, bite me, and take me inside. Please, Mariah, give it all to me, and don't hold back. I need you to love me, just as I am."

"I do," she nearly sobbed out as she silently echoed his plea.

Five

If the pain that had knifed through him minutes ago had been unbearable, the hot slide of blood rushing through him now was pure torture.

Her shaking hand hesitated, fingertips spread through the coarseness of hair, the vulnerability of flesh. Time stopped on a suspended heartbeat before accelerating to a blur as she suddenly delved, fumbled, then held him.

His breath left him completely, while hers, smelling of sweet champagne, fanned his face. Sol was struck with wonder. For a man who had accumulated enough carnal knowledge to fill a library, he was suddenly, inexplicably, on virgin ground.

With no more than Mariah's tentative stroke and curiously awkward squeeze, he felt a heavy throb spear through him and culminate in a tiny spurt of liquid. This sudden slip of control was unbelievable. It was also a damn heady rush. If she kept this up much longer, he'd be consummating their marriage by himself.

"Stop." Sol gripped her wrist tight but she seemed

unwilling or unable to follow his urgent command. Sweat beaded his brow with the effort of restraint as he stared down at the feverish intensity of her unblinking, trancelike gaze. "Mariah, please—let . . . go."

His hand was shaking—hell, he was shaking all over—as he stroked the hair from her temple and felt the rapid pounding of her pulse. His own was out of control, yanked from his ribs and plummeting through the sweet pain threatening to explode in his groin. "What's happening to us?"

"I—don't know." And she didn't. She didn't know anything but the marvelous discovery of the power she held in her hand. Sleek and brutally hard. Pulsing and hot and *alive*. A streaking sensation was overtaking her, causing her womb to contract. "I feel so . . . so strange."

"Yes," he whispered softly. "I feel it too."

Her hand was trapped, lodged between unyielding pants and unyielding flesh. She was pinned by his weight, his searching gaze. She was absorbing him, his scent that was masculine and clean, the subtle shift of his hips that rocked her very bones, and his sounds, harsh breathing sounds that filled her ears and seemed to stroke her most intimate places.

"Is . . . this normal?" she asked.

"Baby, I don't know about you, but I've never experienced anything like this in my life." Sol's low chuckle caught on a ragged groan. "Please, Mariah, take your hand out of my pants, or this is going to be over before it gets started."

"I can't—can't move." Her head lolled to the side, and the carpet was rough against her cheek. She was so sensitized, she felt each nub, each fiber against her skin. "Help me?"

His fingers sought hers, and even that small act became an erotic feast.

Their wedding bands connected. Gold rode upon gold, and their vows were suddenly there between them, a haunting memory of sheer terror, the heartbreak of losing him while the scream of *STAT!* pierced her ears.

"To have and to hold." Tears smarted in her eyes and leaked from the corners. "I never thought I'd hold you like this. I lost you, Sol, and I thought I was dying with you. Don't leave me, never leave me again."

He glided her palm over taut muscle and hard chest covered by a crisp shirt. Then he lifted her hand and pressed his lips to the center of it before running her band of gold against his whiskered cheek.

"Don't cry. I'm here, and we've got the rest of our lives together. You're my wife, Mariah. I'm not close to perfect, and I can be hard." His smile was suggestive and coaxed a small, throaty laugh from her. "But I have some deeply ingrained beliefs, and one of those is that marriage is for life. For all the wild oats I've sown, I can be unfashionably old-fashioned. Fidelity. Respect. Commitment. The whole bit. Maybe I took my vows without realizing they'd stick, but I took them and we're together from this day forward."

"You don't regret it?"

"I did, but not since I laid eyes on you." He fingered his patch, and she felt a quick stab of empathy. Mariah reached up and stroked away his finger to touch the material. "Somehow that feels more personal than when your hand was in my pants," he said quietly. "And that's about as personal as a woman can get."

"But I'm not just any woman." She traced the edge of the patch and her breath caught. She knew what she was about to do and wasn't certain it was wise, but driven by a need to take their intimacy beyond sex, she slid her finger beneath the patch. "I'm your wife."

Sol tensed and grew still with each taut second of her invasion.

The fan of his eyelashes gave way to the smoothness of sealed skin. Carefully she traced the suture, then the place where his eye had been. The other stared down at her with disbelief, warning, and a naked vulnerability that made her heart ache for his loss.

She ached elsewhere too. In the empty region where he pressed but did not enter. Scarcely able to believe she had actually committed such a breach of privacy, Mariah threw caution to the wind and twined both her legs around his as she arched her hips and rubbed. It was decadent and beyond anything she'd dreamed herself capable of, but there she was taking liberties and doing exactly what she wanted. She was shocked at herself, but greatly pleased—*and* most aroused.

"You amaze me," Sol said, curling his fingers around her wrist. "Why did you do it?"

"I wanted to touch you where no one else would."

"You've done that, all right." He firmly removed her hand, then released it. "But in some places that go farther than the eye can see."

"And what do you see in me, Sol?"

"Courage, but a dangerous lack of caution." He made a strangled noise, a rough, inarticulate sound that was between a curse and a groan. "I see a woman I want to take to bed, or better yet, here on the floor. Whether or not you realize it, you just cut through any pretense of politeness I felt obliged to show." A muscle ticked beside his cheek. Naked, unslaked hunger was etched in his face, causing her to realize there would be a price for her reckless courage.

There was an intensity in him that suggested a furious passion. She'd done away with his veneer of gentility. He wanted her, and he wanted her *now*.

Mariah tried to swallow past the tightness in her throat, her fingers fluttering against her neck. Sol brushed them away and stroked the runaway throb.

"Nervous?" he said in a low, probing voice.

"N-no. Of c-course not."

"Liar," he softly accused, while his gaze fixed on her breasts beneath the see-through silk. "Where's your courage, babe? Don't let it desert you in *my* time of need."

Wishing for his tenderness to come back, Mariah blindly reached for a crutch, hoping a trip to the bed might gentle the moment.

Sol grabbed her arm and adrenaline pumped in her muscles, as if she'd picked up the scent of a predator hot on her trail.

"Let's go to, um . . . b-bed." Her voice was thin.

"Too late. You wanted the real me, and now you've got it. This is who I am, and what I am right now is not patient. We're getting naked."

"Please, Sol, don't be angry with me."

"Not angry, just pushed past my limit. You've stripped me to my bare bones. Now it's my turn to put us on even ground. That is what marriage is all about—give and take. Only we do seem to be getting a crash course."

In one smooth movement, he rolled her on top, then gripped the gown that had bunched at her hips, peeled it off, inside out, and flung it aside.

Instinctively, Mariah sat up on his pelvis and crossed her arms over her bare breasts.

"No way." He pried her arms away and held them firmly by her sides while he gazed hungrily at her bare chest. "You wanted to touch me where no one else would, and you did. Now you let me touch you where no else ever will, and at the moment, that's your breasts. By the way, love . . . " He paused. "I think they're beautiful."

He pulled her down until she was leaning over his chest and her breasts hung freely above his mouth.

A strangled yelp of protest escaped her.

"Don't fight me," he warned softly. "No more running for either of us. The dress rehearsal is over, and this is for keeps. Let's make it count." His hand brushed her spine so lightly it brought chills to her skin. And then there was heat, wetness, the sudden stunning feel of a single breast taken almost wholly into his mouth.

Jolts of electric sensation shot through her and she nearly collapsed on his face. He was tasting her, sucking her deep. On and on it went, until she sobbed his name and struck her fist against the floor.

He murmured words that bespoke encouragement, approval, lust—all the things she had begun to feel deep in her bones, which were melting, capitulating to impatient desire.

His masterful handling filled her with unbounded sensation and held her prisoner. Yet at the same time it set her free from all restraint, sending her on a journey to womanly discovery.

She began to rock against him, trying to assuage a strange emptiness inside her that was wonderful, horrible. She was floating up, up. Her body had never been so alive.

In her mindlessness, in the sheer hedonistic delight he gave and she greedily took, Mariah was barely aware that he was staring at her, at the picture of wantonness she made.

"Just look at you there," Sol said fiercely. "So hot for me, just as I am for you. Hungry for more than a taste and . . . I think I did die. This has to be heaven."

Hardly realizing that he was pulling her forward,

guided willingly by the urgency of his hands on her hips, she was shocked to feel his impatient fingers on her panties, his teeth ripping the silk barrier, then his tongue slowly lapping her moist heat.

Mariah's head fell forward and she could scarcely believe what they were doing, what she'd eagerly assented to.

"My word," she moaned. "What are you doing?"

"Exactly what I want, that's what," he mouthed against her, then nipped the inside of her thigh. "Making love to my wife and loving every minute of it, because you want it as much as I do. Don't move, don't think. Just relax and enjoy what we're sharing." He put his mouth back where it had been and let his actions do the rest of the talking.

Disbelieving, Mariah watched him. Could this really be her? Moving and moaning and witnessing this act? It *was* her, she realized, a part of her that she hadn't known existed but had emerged with a ferocity that matched his. A ferocity fueled by want and passion. Passion for him, for life. Wasn't that the secret longing that had driven her to flee from home and into a stranger's arms?

The realization came to her with startling clarity. This was the journey, her chosen path. She was her own person, free to stumble and fall and triumph with this mate she desperately loved.

"I love this," she whispered fervently. "I love you. And I do want it too. Anything. Everything."

He claimed her with his fingers and she took his offering with abandon. This was hers, *theirs!*

Her head fell back, her arms stretched up, her fingertips reached for heaven, and she knew the sheer giddiness of flight. Laughter rolled from her throat and emerged as a victory cry that was throaty, triumphant, sublime.

Six

In answer, he spurred her on with loving words and tender strokes.

"Enough," she finally cried out. "No more, Sol, please."

"Please," he repeated with a lusty growl. "Such a lady in a wanton's body. You couldn't be more perfect for me. Take off my shirt—it's time we got serious."

She'd never undressed a man, never dreamed she would be so eager that she'd tear buttons loose. And she hadn't imagined that this demanding lover—her beloved, her husband—would call this wildness up from her.

"I love your chest, the way you're made," she said as she cast aside his shirt. She stroked through the coarse thatch of hair, then kissed the vivid scar in the middle. "And I love this. Without it, you wouldn't be here, and neither would I."

"If you can love it, then I can live with it." He hooked his thumbs into his pants waist, but before he could pull them off, Mariah stopped him, covering his hands with hers. She'd cut through the obstacle of his patch; now she wanted it all.

"Let me. If you don't mind my help."

His internal struggle showed in the sudden tautness of his features, and she knew a sinking regret that he would refuse her for the sake of false pride.

He traced her cheekbone with an aching tenderness she didn't expect, then cupped her chin and slid his lips back and forth against hers.

"It's not that I don't want your help, Mariah. Never again will I refuse you that. The problem is, I'm not a pretty sight underneath, and I wish that I was. For you. God, how much I wish that—as much as I resent not being able to pick you up and carry you to bed." He rubbed his thumb over the moistness he'd left on her mouth. "Shut your eyes while I take my pants off and pretend I'm what I was when you first cared."

"I can't do that. I care too much. What you were, what I was then, are memories. I want what you are, what we both are. Deny me that and you deprive us both."

A long sigh sifted through his lips and he fell back on his elbows. "All right then. Do it."

She could feel his intense gaze on her as she carefully, gently worked the pants down. The sight of him released was mesmerizing, breathtaking. Temptation and curiosity made her stop undressing him, and she gave in to the need to touch, to stroke, to take this wondrous prize that came to life in her hands.

Holding him tightly, Mariah slid her fingers down velvety-soft skin and was rewarded with an anguished groan. She did it once more, and again he made that beautiful, bestial sound.

What he'd done to her, obliterating her modesty

and making her writhe, she was doing to him now. Nothing she'd ever read had mentioned the thrill of power that came with pleasuring a man.

Mariah glanced up to verify that she was actually capable of this remarkable feat. Sol appeared to be in the throes of torture. How . . . curious. Intriguing. Absolutely delightful.

"You like this, what I'm doing to you, don't you?"

"Sweet heaven, Mariah, what kind of question is that?"

Mariah wasn't about to tell him it was the question of a genius who'd unexpectedly found a wealth of knowledge that she now intended to explore to her heart's content.

"You do," she said decisively. "You like it a lot! And so do I."

"Well, thank God for that."

She continued her exploration, growing braver and more inventive, and each manipulation resulted in increasingly ragged groans from him and answering sighs from her.

Her wings were new, and she was completely intoxicated with the rush of first flight and the realization that she was the master of her fate. In this moment, this room, she could be a fledgling sparrow or a soaring eagle. She made her choice.

"If you liked that," she murmured seductively, "I'm sure you'll love this." She lowered her head and discovered him anew with her mouth.

Suddenly, she felt his hands on either side of her head and heard a hoarse command to stop what she was doing. Refusing to let Sol clip her wings, she bravely continued, only to feel his hand twist into her hair and tug firmly. He gently pulled her up.

"Mariah," he bit out, "get the pants off before I

decide to leave them on and find out what else you learned from Pat Pong's. Or elsewhere."

His stare was heated, raw, and unmistakably possessive. She realized Sol apparently thought she'd had a lot of experience at this, and didn't like it. Her husband had a jealous streak and he didn't want to share her.

Mariah ducked her head to hide a satisfied smile, then worked the pants down. She beheld the desecration of a masterpiece. Once perfect, now permanently marred, his legs were a patchwork quilt of muscles that had been torn apart and pieced back together. How could he even walk with the crutches and bear it? she wondered, fighting quick tears of compassion.

"Damn, don't you cry."

"I can't help it," she whispered brokenly. "I hurt for you." She tenderly kissed his ravaged leg while she caressed the other, which had seen less abuse. "And your strength humbles me. How much pain you must have gone through to come this far." She raised her head and was greeted by a blue-eyed gaze that reflected passion, steely control, then surprise . . . and relief.

"Come here." He reached for her and she clung to him. Nestled in his arms, Mariah buried her face against his neck and wept.

"Save your tears for someone who needs them, love," He rocked her back and forth. "I've got all a man could want."

"You do?" She sniffled. His pat on her back became a long stroke, which ended in a massage of her buttocks.

"I've got you. Now if you really want to ease my pain—" Sol rolled her over. Lying atop her, he pressed himself against her. "This is my only need. To be inside you."

"Then be there."

He pressed harder and she gasped at the invasion, the too-full invasion that somehow wasn't enough.

"Mariah?"

"Don't stop." Her fingernails dug into his shoulders and she arched up.

He retreated. "You should have told me." His rebuke was as gentle as the hands that stroked her hair. "No wonder you . . . God, I must be blind in both eyes. Here, love, hold my hand." He kissed her wedding band and said solemnly, "With this ring, I thee wed."

He wed his body to hers, wooing her with measured thrusts. But she wanted all of him. She loved him, felt it so strongly she breathed the vow again and again. And the words wouldn't stop coming. She was telling him her deepest thoughts, saying he was so tender she wanted to cry, and that she loved him and all his facets, even those she had yet to learn. She'd come so close to losing him. The nightmare of his dying was upon her, and then she was beseeching him. Sol, Sol, make it go away.

"Come home to me, Sol." Her entreaty was frantic, as were her undulating hips. "Please, come home."

"For you, gladly." Sol crushed her lips and entered her mouth with the sleek heat of his tongue.

Pain, such beautiful pain, because he had given it, and in that pain they were sealed shut and made one.

His mouth took the small, sharp cry she couldn't suppress, swallowed it, and sought more. With each crush of chest to breast, each stroke to the tip of her womb, she climbed a dizzying spiral. Then suddenly she was falling, falling into darkness with the rush of hot wind that was his breath and the swirling liquid that was their ecstasy.

They had died, she thought blissfully, died together and emerged entwined in this new life that was full of wonder and promise.

"Home," she cried softly. "I'm finally home."

"Damn if I'm not too." His cracked voice was the sound of a man crying, but without tears. Cradling her face in his hands, he kissed her again and again, tenderly, passionately. "Glory be, if God hasn't cut me some slack and doled out a miracle. He does indeed move in strange and mysterious ways."

"Tell me the miracle." She traced his lips with shaking fingertips. He caught one in his mouth and nipped it.

"The miracle, Mariah, is *you.*"

Sol stroked his eye patch as he studied his sleeping bride huddled against his chest on the bed. He'd thought he knew Mariah from the letters, but it seemed the letters had sold her short. She'd gone from blushing bride to wanton sensualist to sweetly passionate virgin. He felt as if he'd made love to three different women.

If it wasn't for the paralyzing pain in his left leg, he'd take each woman again and again, separately and then collectively. Reaching for the second bottle of champagne, Sol spied his duffel bag. The pain pills were in there. He needed them to silence the stabbing pain the booze had only temporarily dulled.

His lips thinned as he remembered the shock of Mariah's fingertip beneath his patch, followed by his grudging respect for her foolhardy courage. She had struck the invisible wall that had kept him insulated in his private prison, had shattered the brittle shell.

Mariah's strength had managed to summon his own. Where had it been? How had he let himself fall into the trap of self-pity she had zeroed in on with unerring accuracy?

Thrusting the sheet aside, Sol was careful not to waken her as he grabbed his crutches and headed for the bag. His grip tightened around the vial of pills when he found it. Before he could change his mind, he went to the toilet and flushed his supply of borrowed relief with a decisiveness that marked the person he had once been and was now reclaiming.

With a sense of resolve, he watched the medication make its swirling voyage into the sewer.

Returning to Mariah, he shut his mind to the pain and gritted his teeth in determination. He *would* walk again, tall and sure in his steps. He gave himself six months to burn the crutches and carry Mariah to bed.

"Thank you," he said to her sleepy murmurings, then settled her questing hand over his groin. "You gave this back to me, and more. Whatever makes you tick escapes me, but you're in a league of your own."

Sol was more than a little confused and a whole lot intrigued. As he continued to study her, he puzzled over an unexpected element in their relationship. Despite her innocence, she'd forged heedlessly forward, as if embarking on a brave new world she couldn't get enough of. Their lovemaking had sucked him in with her, and there he had regained his footing.

As he tucked the covers around her, a niggling suspicion escalated to an affirmation.

He was falling in love with his wife.

Seven

"We're home," LaVerne announced.

Mariah craned her neck, eager for a view of the farmhouse, but all she saw were rolling green pastures and cornfields as far as the eye could see. Huge trees lined the road, forming a lush tunnel of green. The scenery was breathtaking, picture-postcard perfect. With a rush of excitement, she sent a silent prayer of thanks for this serene haven that was now her home.

"Where is the house?" she asked.

"Down the road a piece," Herbert answered.

Sol leaned closer and made a sweeping gesture with his hand. "This is our land." His breath tickled her neck and warmth trickled through her. "Yours too, Mariah."

She turned and was greeted by his watchful gaze. His words flowed through her while the silence sizzled with shared intimate memories. Invisible fingers of heat stoked the fire neither seemed able, or inclined, to bank.

His arm brushed her breast as he reached past her

to lower the window, and she felt an immediate spark ignite from the contact. A sensual cast darkened his features and his arm lingered to subtly press possessively against her.

Anticipating a kiss and suddenly in dire need of one, Mariah moistened her lips. Sol's attention was on the flick of her tongue when the car hit a bump. He grimaced.

He was hurting, she knew, just as she knew he wouldn't admit to the pain. Mariah laid her hand across his leg and soothingly stroked, wishing more than anything that she could take his pain into herself, or at least share it and lessen his burden, just as he shared his body and his home with her.

Sol's hand covered hers and squeezed. This they shared too, this closeness that didn't need words. And longing. She felt its forceful pull and she gazed at him with desire. There was a small nick in the strong, shaven jaw that carried his marvelous scent, and the capable fingers interlocking with hers were strong. Lord, he was sexy. *And all hers.*

"I can't wait to see the whole spread," she said as anticipation heightened. "Will you show me all the places you played in while growing up?"

"After I show you around our house and all the places I'd like to play in now that I'm grown up and have a playmate."

"Sol, shhh." Mariah glanced anxiously at the front seat.

Sol's sudden laughter made LaVerne turn around. "It's good to hear you laugh, son."

"Feels good too, Ma."

LaVerne smiled approvingly at him, and then at Mariah, before turning back. With a wolfish grin, he murmured, "But not half as good as you feel under me. Or beside me."

Color bloomed in her cheeks, from pleasure and mild embarrassment. Heavens, but he was direct, and obviously amused by her discomfort. Miss Lilah would be shocked out of her finishing-school finesse. And her parents, the epitome of propriety, would be horrified if they knew that their daughter, instead of getting ready for medical school, had gone wild over a man who made lewd remarks.

After three days, three glorious days, during which she'd blocked out everything but honeymoon passion, reality had finally intruded on her bliss. Staring out the window and glimpsing the high roof of a barn, Mariah mentally shook herself. So what if something foul was eventually due to hit the fan? *This* was her home now. Sol was her husband. Life was what she made it, and she would seize it, wallow in it, and relish each experience.

The wind caught at her hair and she shook it out. Turning her face to the sun, she felt its rays in every pore of her skin. One barn became two, then three, and beyond those she could make out several tall cylindrical buildings and a huge white house. It was almost palatial in size, old but well maintained and seeming to breathe with a life of its own.

She felt the tug of Sol's fingers in her hair, and swung around to face him.

"I'll always be beside you," she vowed fiercely. "And I can't wait to see the cottage, to make it *our* home."

"You won't have to wait." He gave her a quick, hard kiss. "We're here, babe. Welcome home."

The car rolled to a stop across the street from the house, and Sol reached past her to open the door. She scooted out, feeling the rise of great expectations. She didn't let herself look right away, but closed her eyes and mentally drew the picture Sol had painted—a modest cottage on a small lot used by foremen past. Nothing impressive, but sufficient.

Feeling the pressure of his palms on her shoulders, Mariah opened her eyes. She blinked, then blinked again. No, she hadn't imagined the carefully tended lawn teeming with flowers blooming in a riot of vivid colors, or the house that sat like a sparkling gem in the middle.

"Sol." She breathed his name, then inhaled the heady mixture of flowers, grass, and pure country air. "It's absolutely beautiful."

"Beautiful?" He sounded surprised. "It's been here for as long as I can remember, and I never thought the place more than a hideout when Dad had a list of chores I didn't want to do on Saturday mornings."

"You're wrong. It's so much more than that." Mariah moved one of his hands from her shoulder to her waist. Sol brought both arms around her and hugged her close, his chin nuzzling her head. "You're too close to it, that's all. I wish you could see through my eyes."

"So do I. Tell me what you see."

A lush smile brimmed from her lips to her eyes, which were suddenly moist. Mariah spread her arms, then hugged herself as if she were embracing the vision before her.

"I see lacy gingerbread fretwork dripping like snowflakes from a gabled roof. The wraparound porch looks like a floating oasis, and that white wicker swing is just begging me to curl up in the middle with an icy glass of tea and a book. The awnings are like sleepy lids over pane-glass-window eyes. And the picket fence looks like Tom Sawyer's dupes just put on the last coat of whitewash." She pried her gaze from the house to beam up at Sol. "I half expect Hansel and Gretel to come out any minute. That was always my favorite illustration in the storybooks—and you just gave it to me."

Sol studied Mariah's intent, glowing face, and felt something stir in his chest. He was taken aback by her reaction; Desiree had always turned her spoiled nose up at the thought of living there when they'd been kids pretending to be married.

Tilting Mariah's chin up, Sol absorbed her beatific expression. His wife had class, brains, a tender heart, and a body that wouldn't quit. Which only made him wonder why she sidestepped certain questions. How much was she hiding from him?

He found it hard to imagine her capable of deceit as he felt himself sinking deep, drowning in those doe-brown eyes that glistened with openness, gratitude, joy. Why, she looked as if he'd just given her Buckingham Palace. Strange, since she came from purebred stock. Not that she'd told him, but he'd put the signs together and figured that out. Among other things.

Yep. Mariah was a mystery he was itching to unveil.

"Why don't you go find out if that swing's as comfortable as it looks while Dad hauls out the luggage and I get the keys."

"You're sure?" She glanced wistfully at the house. "I can wait for you."

"No you can't." He swatted her playfully on the rump and she gasped, then looked to see if his parents, who were busy unlocking the trunk, had noticed. Sol chuckled heartily. Spitfire kitten or Miss Priss, she could make him laugh. Mariah was a tonic, and the more he drank of her, the more he wanted. Fact was, he was downright crazy about her, and getting crazier by the day. Which he had to be, since he'd decided that wasn't a picture of her she'd sent him and she couldn't lie worth beans.

"Go on, you," he said, and gave her a slight push. "Get outta here and warm those sweet little buns on the swing that's begging you to curl up in it. Of course, knowing just how sweet they are, I'd be tempted to beg too."

"You're depraved." She balanced on tiptoe and kissed him on the cheek. "And I wouldn't have you any other way."

With that, she spun around and all but skipped down the cobblestone walk. Had he not been watching, he expected she would have pirouetted and hopscotched to the picket fence, where she now swung the gate back and forth as if hypnotized by the movement.

"Well? What does your wife think of her new home, Sol?" he heard his mother ask.

"I think you can guess with no more than a look." Sol put his arm around her shoulders as he watched Mariah slowly pivot. Her head fell back and she seemed to be saying something to the towering trees. He'd climbed those same trees as a boy, had imagined he could see exotic countries where life was a great adventure, not pastures filled with more cows than people.

"She's special, son. Under the circumstances, I had my misgivings, but I'm glad to say they weren't warranted. You chose well."

"Mariah's something else, all right. There's still a lot I have to learn about her, but that works both ways and we've got plenty of time to find each other out."

"Take it from me—you never stop learning about the people you love. We all change, and that's part of what keeps a marriage alive." They watched as

Mariah walked her fingertips up the curved stone banister, then traced the swirling wood column that supported the porch's ceiling. "Do you love her?"

"Fact is, I think I do. If not, I'm close to it."

"Then you know the most important thing there is to know about her. Whatever those mysteries are that your brain is turning this way and that—such as the fact that she changes the subject whenever her parents get mentioned—they'll all come to light soon enough."

"Don't I guess. But I'm giving her a little time to tell me herself before I start digging around for the truth. For now, it's enough to know that she's of legal marrying age and that dishonesty doesn't set well with her. Whatever her reasons, I'm sure they're justified. And it won't be long before she can't stand keeping them to herself. As it is, I don't expect to end up on the wrong side of a gun, and I need her in my life. Enough that I'm willing to bide my time and put up with some subterfuge—for now, anyway."

LaVerne nodded. "Try to be patient. She loves you."

"So she says. And I believe that's true."

"Then I'll hold my tongue and try not to meddle. I'm your mother, Sol, and so I'm selfish, because I see how much that girl has done for my boy."

"That she has." His gaze settled on his too-young wife. Young and full of a love for life he'd lost but was rediscovering because of her. "I believe her folks really are in Europe, though I doubt they have any idea she's here."

"*You're* here. After all these years, you've come home. I just wish it hadn't taken a grenade to send you back. I'm sorry for your loss, son, but I'd be a liar to say I'm not happy to have you return, no matter what. This is where you belong. Our heritage is here and I just wish to God you loved this land as much as we do."

"Maybe I will, Ma. I've hurt you and Dad deep, but I'm beginning to think that grenade knocked some sense into my brain. Nothing looks quite the same."

"How's that?" LaVerne asked hopefully.

Sol watched as Mariah settled into the wicker swing and blew him a kiss before stretching her arms out on either side and rocking.

Thrusting his crutches forward, he turned back long enough to smile at his mother. But not just any smile. A smile as content as that of an engorged cow that had just gotten milked.

"It looks different from someone else's perspective," he said, then nodded toward his wife. "After years of traveling the globe, I'm finally seeing the world . . . through Mariah's eyes."

After hanging up her last article of clothing in the cedar closet, Mariah turned to see Sol agitatedly finger-drumming on a pine Shaker nightstand. He got up from the filigreed white iron bed and went to stare out a window, its lace curtains dancing in the fragrant breeze.

"What's wrong, Sol?" Laying her cheek against his tense back, she felt the heat of his skin through the crisp cotton shirt. "You're upset about something."

"You're right, Mariah. Something is bothering me." His head fell forward and she heard a snort of frustration that caused her to stiffen. Had she bungled an explanation? Had he noticed that without makeup she looked as young as she was? Her mind spun with incriminating scenarios and she knew a sudden, frantic fear of exposure.

"I wish—" She wished she were ten years older.

More confident in her newly realized persona. Taking a shallow breath, she forced herself to be as brave as she longed to be. "I wish you would tell me what's on your mind."

"You." He shook his head and her stomach twisted. "It bothers me that I couldn't carry you over the threshold."

Relief washed through her. She slumped against his back and possessively fanned her hands over his chest. His heart was a steady throb that coursed through her fingertips and spread through her veins, matching the beat of her pulse.

"I know it's just an outdated ritual," he said. "But it's a thorn in my side all the same, a reminder that I can't do something as simple as carrying my woman in my arms." Sol leaned against the window frame and pressed his hands over hers. "Does that seem trivial to you?"

"Far from it." Not for the first time, she was warmed by his desire for her opinion. What she thought mattered to him, in a way that had nothing to do with intellect and everything to do with soul. "I'm touched that carrying me over the threshold means that much to you. And because it means that much, it's even better than you actually doing it."

The tenseness of his back eased, then he turned and brought her into his arms.

"I don't know how you do it, lady, but you always manage to say what I need to hear." His jaw tightened and he got a very determined look on his face. "I'm going to carry you over that threshold one day. As God is my witness, I will."

"Then I believe it too. The mind is a very powerful tool, and yours seems to be stronger than most. Studies have been done that prove—" Mariah stopped short. She'd been about to quote statistics, cases, miracles, comparisons of standard courses of therapy to little-known practices. A concise documentation of volumes of study that most doctors would have been hard pressed to detail.

The silence lengthened, as did Sol's puzzled gaze. Managing a slight shrug, she said simply, "I learned in college that attitude has a lot to do with healing. So if you're determined to throw away those crutches, there's a much better chance that you will walk with that point of view."

His brow furrowed while he studied her a little longer; the urge to dart out the door was strong, but she managed to give him an encouraging smile instead.

"Why do I get the feeling that you're smart as a whip but you try not to let it show? Surely you're not one of those gals who think men find dimwits more attractive than a woman with a sharp mind, are you?" He speared both hands into her hair and held her head.

Mariah endured his scrutiny, tried to ignore the stunning sensual heat that radiated from his fingers.

"I—I had reason to think being too smart intimidated men." She felt him release her head, only to lay his palms on her throat, then trail a path over her breasts down to her hips, where he began to work up her skirt. "It doesn't bother you if I'm . . . a fast learner?"

"No. In fact, you'd better learn fast that I think intelligence is sexy as hell. I can't wait to find out what's in that head of yours—motivations, fantasies, secrets. What makes you"—he pulled her flush against him—"*tick.*"

Eight

"Mind if we rest a bit, babe?" Leaning against a fence post, Sol gritted his teeth in an effort to disguise the pain he was battling. "It's a long walk back and I'm—"

"Hurting. Why didn't you say something sooner?" Tracing his jaw, she shook her head. "It's my fault, for getting so caught up with my own pleasure. If I hadn't been so excited to see your land, I would have realized. I'm sorry, Sol. I hate to see you hurt."

"I know that, and don't you dare go blaming yourself. We've been here nearly a week and not once have you asked to go past the barns. You've been patient, and it means a lot to me that you didn't want anyone else to show you around."

"I'm glad I waited." Mariah made a sweeping gesture that encompassed the surrounding area, and he felt a sense of oneness with her and this place in which his roots ran deep. As always, those roots tugged at him. But what had once felt like tentacles tangling around his feet now seemed more and more a welcome caress.

"It's so beautiful here," she said with awe. "There's something uncomplicated and honest and rich about this land. How lucky you were to grow up with it. And how lucky I am to share it." Her face was impassioned, her whispered words fierce. "Thank you, Sol. Thank you."

"Wrong, Mariah. It's me who's thanking you." He caught her hand and focused on the wedding band, shutting out his pain by shuffling through frame-by-frame images of Mariah during their walk.

Her floppy straw hat caught by the wind and somersaulting over a thick pasture of grass. Grass that he'd never realized was so lush and vibrantly green until she'd chased through it, peasant skirt flying, tangling about her legs as she laughed up at the sky. And why hadn't he noticed how sweet the wildflowers smelled until she'd tickled one under his nose, or that dandelions were more than a nuisance? They were floating dreams, she'd said, blowing them from her lips.

And the cows. Those bovine grass munchers he'd never considered more than dumb udders to be milked were suddenly pets that needed naming according to their dispositions. He saw her hesitantly touching their short, coarse hair, then stroking the damn creatures as if they were sleek pussycats. Her quick jerk as one took some hay from her hand, her giggles as she grew bolder and they were eating out of her hand.

Feeling the stabs of pain abate, Sol leaned his crutches against the fence. When one fell, he automatically stooped to retrieve it. A sharp curse exploded from his lips as he remained bent at the knee.

"I'll get it." Mariah crouched down and retrieved the crutch, a simple feat that for now was impossible for him. While Sol swallowed equal measures of frustration and ache, she fixed him with a level stare.

"I live with you, Sol. I wake up in the night and hear you cursing while you pace the porch. When I come out, you paste on a smile that looks like a grimace before you tell me to go back to sleep because you've got insomnia. If it was insomnia, you'd be drinking warm milk instead of taking a swig from a flask. You're in pain almost constantly, and you won't take anything other than a few nips to deal with it. Why not?"

"Because that's my decision," he snapped, immediately regretting his tone. Wincing, he straightened and softened his voice. "I don't need pills, Mariah. I need your company, your support."

"You need them all, Sol. Enduring pain doesn't make you more of a man, just as taking something for it doesn't make you less of one."

"Maybe. Maybe not. The point is, the pain gives me something to fight. One of us is going to win, and I don't lose easy."

He touched his eye patch, hating the loss it covered yet determined to accept it as a fact of life.

"I know you don't lose easy, Sol. For that reason, I can't help but wonder why you didn't accept a glass eye in exchange for what was rightfully yours."

"Because it's fake. I was tempted, believe me, to look as good as I could, in the hope that you'd want to keep me. But I decided that whether or not you stayed should be based on who I truly am, not a glamorized version."

He could almost see the wheels turning in her pretty little head, and knew she debated whether he was sending her an underlying message.

"I stayed, and still you keep your patch, which is perfectly fine. But to refuse some help for the pain?

What do you have to prove, besides the fact that you can best it?"

"This time, Mariah, try to see through my eye. A glass one is artificial, so I shun it for a patch. The pills are just as artificial. I am who I am, so I don't want either. Depending on false securities is as much of a crutch as these pieces of wood I resent leaning on."

"I disagree. If you hurt, you hurt. Time helps; believe me, I know."

"And how would you know that?"

She did it again! Got that shuttered look on her face and glanced away. He knew it as surely as he breathed—Mariah had some medical know-how that went beyond college and that she didn't want to spill. He couldn't figure it. She looked too young to even have a college degree, much less a professional opinion.

"I . . . well, I was in an accident once. Nothing as severe as what you've gone through, but enough that I needed medication until I could deal with my injury alone."

"And what might that injury have been?"

She hesitated, biting her bottom lip. A lip he'd like to bite himself, suck into his mouth, and ravage until she surrendered her secrets.

"A dislocated shoulder. A—a broken leg, too."

The little liar. Did she actually think he'd fallen off the turnip truck yesterday? Mariah was as transparent as plastic wrap, and because she was so obviously unschooled in the art of deception, he granted her a reprieve—after making her squirm a full minute with a narrow-eyed stare.

"You know, Mariah, honesty's a big thing with me. Because of that, I'm going to tell you another reason I flushed those painkillers." It wasn't easy to disclose his masculine insecurities, but maybe, just maybe, she'd confess if he did. "Until I laid eyes—or rather, eye—on you, I had reason to doubt if I could get it up."

Her startled gasp at his bluntness coaxed an inner smile in Sol. Mariah had been sheltered, and expanding her education had become a rejuvenating kick for him.

"You heard right. That damn grenade took more than just a good chunk of my leg. It took my self-confidence, my goals, and my sex drive right along with it. Embarrassing as it was, I asked the doctors—you know, *smart* people who know a *lot* about *medicine*—if I'd had my baby-making gears stripped in the accident. Why no, they said, it could be the medicine."

Mariah turned a funny color before slumping against the fence. Whether it was his innuendo about her medical background, or his frankness, or both, he wasn't sure. But whatever it was, he liked getting under her skin since she'd dug beneath his.

"I had no idea," she finally said in a breathy voice. "Especially since you were so—well, I mean . . ." She swallowed hard. "You've certainly proven that you're not im-impotent."

"You've got that right, babe. In fact, I'm suddenly feeling randier than hell." He moved against her and softly commanded, "Turn around, Mariah. I want you to latch on to that fence and hold it as tight as you hold me inside."

Sol was amazed that she could be all wide eyes and hand-covered breasts now when they'd tangled like animals in heat the night before. Her surprise and modesty only intensified the arousal that was shouting down the pain, and increased his fixation on this walking contradiction of a wife.

"Why the fence?"

"I think that's apparent, love." He lingered over the endearment, a word that had never held so much meaning for him before. He was in love, and falling harder by the minute, but that was a declaration he didn't take lightly, and until he was certain the endearment would have to make do. "The reason you're grabbing that wood is so I can reassure myself I did the right thing when I flushed those pills and that what we shared on our honeymoon was no fluke."

"Sol, you're—"

"Hot for you. Crazy about you. Now I want to make you a little crazy too."

"But we're in an open pasture," she protested.

"So what?"

"So *what*? Someone could find us!"

"We're in the middle of nowhere and you're worried about being discreet? The way you act sometimes makes me wonder how you were raised." When she looked away, Sol caught her chin and forced her to face him. His patience was wearing a little thin; he was getting few answers. "Didn't your parents ever go to their bedroom and shut the door in the middle of the day?"

"Of course not!" Mariah sniffed, her nose tilting up regally as she came to her parents' defense. "But just because they're reserved doesn't mean they aren't fond of each other."

"Fond of each other? People are fond of their pets, their cousins, maybe even a favorite pair of old shoes. But who the hell wants to be 'fond' of someone they fight with, make love to, and stay up all night with when they've got a sick child? Mariah, if 'fond' ever describes what we feel for each other, I'll be real worried about our marriage."

Several emotions flashed across her face, and he craved to get into that head of hers. In fact, it downright galled him that she kept things locked away he couldn't get at, when he'd let her into places in himself no one had ever been.

"What are you thinking?" he demanded.

"About us, what brought us together. I'm thinking about the changing of the seasons."

"What do seasons have to do with us?"

"Everything. The Bible says there's a time, a season, for every purpose under heaven." Slowly, deliberately, she placed a hand on the fence. "What you said about fondness is true. While it's enough for my parents, it's not half enough for me, for us. And it certainly doesn't describe what I'm feeling now."

"And what might that be?"

"Read my mind."

"Believe me, I'd love nothing better." If she could have read his, what would she think of his calculated reason for what he was about to do?

Dipping a fingertip into the elastic neck of her peasant blouse, Sol was rewarded with the sensual droop of her eyelids. Lower and lower he urged the elastic, brushing her skin with a finger that moved back and forth. He paused to stroke her nipples, until she gripped his wrist and tugged the blouse down beneath the weight of her breasts.

"The fence?" he prompted.

Mariah turned and secured both hands to the weathered wood. "Did you help build this?"

"I did. Just before my sophomore year in college." *When I was just about your age, little lady,* he thought. "Why do you ask?"

"Because it feels strong, solid. Like you." Her breath caught sharply when he grabbed her skirt and gathered it in his fist until it hiked up to her waist. Pulling the fabric through the space between two posts, he wrapped it around twice, then secured a double knot.

Mariah looked at the skirt that locked her to the fence, then at him. Sol surveyed his handiwork before meeting her gaze in silent challenge. Mariah had a few things to learn about him and their relationship; he was eager to get this lesson under way.

She wet her lips uncertainly, then asked, "Why did you do that?"

"Why did you let me?"

"Because . . . I don't know."

"Curiosity?" he suggested. "The sort that *inquiring minds* are compelled to satisfy?"

"Maybe." Her eyes narrowed. "Maybe it's more, such as trying to understand your purpose. You do have a purpose in everything you do, don't you, Sol? This conversation, the fence . . ."

"Very good, Mariah. You're extremely astute, and you already know me better than most." He flicked open the button on his jeans and slid the zipper down. "You're not afraid?"

"Of course not. Why should I be?"

"Since we're still getting to know each other, how do you know I'm not displaying some deviant behavior, now that I have you alone in the middle of nowhere and no one can hear you scream? Or that I won't leave you tied up while I go off alone? By the time you freed yourself, I'd be out of sight. You could wander around lost until it was dark, and end up sleeping outside, with wild animals and no shelter."

"That's ridiculous. You'd never do anything like that."

"But how do you know?"

"Because . . . because I trust you."

Sol nodded in approval. "Now you have your answer as to why I did this, and you've given me yours—the one I'd hoped for, no less."

Comprehension dawned in her eyes, eyes that followed the jeans he was slowly taking off. Mariah reached to touch him. Sol caught her hand and firmly replaced it on the fence.

"You just broke a rule, love."

"A rule? Since when did we have rules?"

"Since I decided we need to play a little game." Edging behind her, he wound her hair around his hand and gently tugged until her head rested against his shoulder. "It's a grown-up game for two players—you and me. The object is trust. You have to give it, and I have to promise not to abuse it. If either of us breaks that rule, the game is forfeited and we both lose. Understand?"

Sol watched closely for her reaction. Her eyes were wary, her uneven voice cautious. "First I want to know the rest of the rules."

"They're simple. I'm going to make love to you while we talk. And as we talk, you won't try to untie yourself from the fence."

"Why?"

"Because you trust me. Second rule—"

"I'm not sure that I like this game. It's a head game, Sol."

"Exactly." He pressed his lips to her head. "And this game isn't over until I get into yours."

Nine

She had the look of a cornered animal, frantic to get away but stunned into immobility. He could feel a fine tremble slither from her back to his chest, and hastened to reassure her.

"Don't worry, I'll be careful. Remember, I can't violate your trust. Now give me enough of it to let me do all the touching. Lay your head against the knot on the fence, Mariah."

When she hesitated, he gently urged her forehead to do his bidding, then stroked her hair away from her neck and trailed his lips against her nape. He covered her left hand with his.

"Comfy?" he whispered. When she stiffly nodded, he softly clucked his tongue. "Mariah, my idea of talking isn't a one-way conversation."

"Yes," she said hesitantly. "Yes, I'm comfortable."

"Ah, that's good. Are your eyes shut?"

"No."

"Then close them for me. In fact, close everything out but my voice and my hands on your skin."

"What do you want to . . . talk about?" she said anxiously.

Damn, he thought. She was wound as tight as a yo-yo, and unless she relaxed, he wasn't going to accomplish a thing.

Seeking to heat her up enough to melt those infuriating defenses, Sol nuzzled her neck while his right hand did enough exploring for two. He roamed from her throat to her breasts to her cleft. Once he felt the melting moisture and her boneless slump against the fence, he secured himself between her, then pressed her legs closed. Mariah inhaled sharply, and he increased the teasing pressure.

"What I want to talk about is us," he said, smooth as worn leather.

"What about . . . us?"

Sol felt the clench of her hand beneath his, the slight movement of her hips working to get closer.

"The way we fit, when we come from such different backgrounds. I've come to realize how little I really know about yours, though I gather it's a far cry from mine. Isn't it?" When she made a muffled sound of assent, he pressed on. "Mariah? I asked you an important question. Please answer."

"Yes," she whispered. "Yes. You have so much here that . . . that I want. That I need."

"And I want you to have it." Sol groaned when she reached between her legs. Unless he was careful, she would beat him at his own seductive game of trust. He quickly yanked her hand away and curved it over the post. "Don't forget the rule. I do all the touching."

"Your rule isn't fair," she moaned.

He tightened his grip. *All's fair in love and war, babe, and I think we're dealing with a little of both here.* He kept the thought to himself, as well as the knowledge that he had no intentions of fighting fair at all. Ignoring her accusation, Sol went for the jugular.

"Today was very special for me, Mariah. The truth

is, I never appreciated what I had here, until you did."
He could feel her immediate softening, the gentle lull
that heralded trust. "And it is a haven, isn't it?"

"I do love this place," she said haltingly. "How
could anyone not? And . . . and—*ah!*"

"Easy," he said, heightening her want by entering
her. "It's easy not to love this farm if you want more
from life than rising before dawn and being tied to a
rigid schedule. It's easy if you're a boy dreaming of
adventure and exotic people and places." He was
moving inside her fast, then slowly, his thrusts deep,
then shallow. "But you've been to such places, haven't you, love? Europe. The Orient. *Pat Pong's.*"

"Why do you . . . keep bringing that up?" She
was moving her forehead back and forth against
the knot, and he wondered if she was wiping away
the sweat of good sex or bad nerves. "Don't you
believe me? Don't you—*oh God!*"

Sol replied with a hard thrust. Oh yeah, he believed her, the same way he believed if she was
twenty-four he was still a plebe in the Marines. He
believed her, just as he swallowed all her tales of
travel after she'd visited the library last week. The
woman had become a walking, talking travelogue.

Mariah was wrong if she thought for a minute
he wasn't on to her, but she had been right about
one thing: This was a head game. And guilt trips were
trump cards.

"Why, of course I believe you, baby," he said,
sincerity oozing from every word. "After all, we're
straight with each other, right?" Sol smiled grimly
when he heard her low groan. "I trust you implicitly.
And I expect you to do the same for me. You're doing
it beautifully now, by the way. Hands spread, legs
and heart and mind open to me—me, your husband,
who would never deceive you or compromise our

trust, because that means more to me than appearances, personal insecurities, or our past lives. And I know you must feel the same way too."

Through his narrowed vision he saw her shudder, and as he toyed with her nipples, he imagined himself suckling them, just like a newborn infant. *Their* baby, to make up for the one he'd lost.

Figuring he'd heaped sufficient guilt on her, Sol decided to show a little mercy.

"Aren't you loving this, Mariah? Getting to know each other better every day is the most exciting adventure of my life. And I have had more than a few."

Just as he'd expected, she was quick to seize the out he offered.

"You've had enough adventures to be content now?"

"More content than I ever believed possible. He nudged her to the fence and pressed against her womanhood. Once she cried out and he was assured of her sustained pleasure, Sol grabbed on to the rail for support. He could feel himself weakening. Beads of sweat bathed his forehead, which he rested next to hers.

"Now that we're assured that I've seen enough of the world to appease my appetites for a lifetime, let's talk about you." Their breaths mingled hotly; his roughened cheek rubbed against the softness of hers. "You like this, don't you?"

"Yes. Yes! What are you doing? What game are you *really* playing with me?"

"Hide-and-seek, it seems." Sol eased up on his thrusting. "Or maybe Twenty-One Questions. First off, have you seen enough of the world to settle on the likes of me?"

"Yes," she cried. "Are you blind? Can't you see how much you mean to me?"

"I'd be a fool not to, and I've been a fool too long.

Next question: Why are you willing to be with me when you've never been with another man?"

"Because you see me, the *real* me, as no else ever has, ever could. Or ever will." The gyration of her torso, the internal clench of her muscles and cry of his name gave credence to her answer.

For now, it was enough for him. As he stroked his wife's bent head, he spent his seed and collapsed over her. She took his weight without complaint. Not for the first time he was struck by her strength, her softness.

"I do see you as you are," he groaned beside her ear, then nursed the fleshy lobe before taking her wedding band between his teeth and gently pulling it.

"Tell me what you see," she pleaded.

"I see a lot, Mariah. Maybe more than you see yourself. I think of you as a steel magnolia. A perfect companion who's slowly repairing the dents in my battered armor."

She was crying. Her shuddering sobs vibrated through to his chest and melted his heart. Apparently someone or something had driven her from her home and into his arms, someone or something that had refused to see her for the warm, sensitive individual she was. That seemed to be the crux of her problem, and doubtless the reason for her flimsy lies.

Wondering how anyone could sell her short, he soothed her with tender strokes. "Can I do anything to make it better, Mariah?"

"No. You make it too good, that's the whole damn problem."

Sol frowned. Her answer wasn't the one he'd hoped for. Had his intention to establish their marriage as one based on honesty and trust caused her to bury her secrets even deeper so she could live up to his expectations? He'd played dirty, but only because he'd been so desperate to get rid of her farce.

For a moment, he debated. Should he push, lay the bones bare while she was close to defenseless? Or back off and give her time to find the answers for herself? Trust. He decided he should show some in her, practice what he'd preached.

"Cry it out," he whispered. "Just cry it out, baby."

"I'm not a baby. And I'm not crying," she insisted while swiping at her cheeks. Sol had to admire the way she kept a stiff upper lip while she fumbled with the knot on her skirt. She clawed at the fabric, striking her fist against the fence when it wouldn't give way. "Untie me," she pleaded, then demanded.

"Shhh, shhh," he whispered beside her ear. "Trust me. Trust yourself. We can't come into our own until you do both, Mariah. Now watch, and think of us." With agile and determined fingertips, he worked the binding loose. "This is the fabric of our lives, bound tight by vows and trust."

He wiped the wetness from her face with the material. She wouldn't look at him, just continued to face the wood post. "And the fence?" she asked hesitantly.

"It weathers the elements. Rain or shine, it remains solid because it's planted firmly in the ground. Even the stormiest gale can't uproot it, because it connects with supports that go deep enough to withstand the hardest blow." He released her skirt and let it flutter from his fingertips and into the cool wind.

Time, she'd said, helped to heal wounds. So did truth. He wanted her, *needed* her, enough to provide the two of them with both.

"Mrs. Standish," he said firmly, "you are my woman. My wife. You're tearing me apart and putting me back together until sometimes I don't even recognize myself. Remember that and think about it."

Whether it was his vow, the deepness of commitment he'd tried to convey, or his emotional plundering that had gotten to her, he wasn't sure. But she was sniffling and wiping her nose against her arm, then cursing in a very unladylike way when, as she bent down to smooth her skirt, a crutch hit her head.

Sol tried to grab it, and their hands met. When she came up, she was rubbing her head. A laugh caught in her throat. She seemed in need of comic relief to patch herself back together.

What a woman. He'd turned her inside out, and she'd definitely returned the questionable favor.

Sol thrust the crutch aside, then slumped against the fence. For once, he wasn't inclined to hide his pain or exhaustion or just what he wanted from her.

"I've got one last question. What am *I* to you? An escape, a turn-on, a great adventure?"

"You're all those things. And more, so much more."

"I want to hear the 'more.'"

"You're my mate, my lover, my friend."

"In that case . . ." He held out his arms and she hugged him tightly. "That's what I wanted. You to hold me . . . and trust me."

"One you've got, and the other I'm learning."

"Well, seeing that patience isn't one of my stronger suits, I'm counting on you being a fast learner."

"There is something I've learned today." She threaded her fingers into his hair, then pulled him down for a scorching kiss. "You're an amazing man, Sol Standish. You say things without saying them, and I do hear you, even in your silence. We share a silent language, you know."

"That we do, love." His smile was warm, intimate. "What should we dub this private dialogue of ours?"

"That's easy," she said softly. "Heart-speak."

Ten

"One more picture, and this roll's done."

"Sol," Mariah groaned. "You must have gone through ten rolls by now."

"So, humor me and I'll give you a break for a few days."

"On one condition. You tell me why you enlisted in the Marines when you had a degree in photojournalism."

As he adjusted the zoom lens, she heard him sigh. "Okay. Patriotism is a big thing with my family, so joining up was an acceptable way out of here. I think my parents figured once I got some wanderlust out of my system, I'd come back home. What they didn't count on was me reenlisting. That was a sore spot with us for a long time."

Sol waved her to the barn gate and checked the filtered interior lighting. Besse, the cow Mariah had adopted as a pet, and who was expecting any day now, nudged her through the wood slat of a pen. There were ten pens in this barn, along with rows and rows of cattle lined up in separate stalls.

Mariah was still amazed that each one ate over eighty pounds of grain a day, and drank a staggering amount of water. Old MacDonald had nothing on the Standishes, she thought wryly. It took fifteen men to feed and milk the livestock, hooking up udders to suction tubes every twelve hours so that the milk flowed through a hose and into a huge refrigerated tank.

"Now that you're here to help, has the sore spot gone away?" she asked. They all worked hard, but especially Sol and Herbert, baling hay, plying the land with tractors.

"Some, but not completely. A breach that big doesn't mend overnight," he said quietly. "I regret hurting them—betraying them, but the decisions I made to strike out on my own were right at the time." He paused. "Know what I mean?"

"Yes, I do." He couldn't know how completely she related—at least, she didn't think so. "Do you think parents ever get over it, when they see their children's need for independence as betrayal?"

Sol hesitated, as if carefully considering his response. "I think, Mariah, that anyone who loves another person has to put his own needs aside sometimes. The urge to hold too tight can be strong, and it's a risky deal. Suffocating a loved one is self-defeating and selfish. I guess the best anyone can hope for is to keep the reins loose enough that betrayal doesn't become necessary in a relationship. That means a relationship based on trust. And honesty."

Trust and honesty. Two words he used a lot and she'd shown precious little of. Each time he said them, they taunted her cruelly. Their silent language had become rife with contradictions that confused her. He would say one thing while she sensed he meant another. And he was given to seemingly subtle actions that struck her as brash. Such as his making a show of replacing Beth's picture in his wallet with a recent one he'd taken of her, then hanging Beth's picture alongside a family portrait and some honeymoon candids in their hallway.

The suspense was killing her. Why didn't he just confront her if he guessed the truth, instead of shading everything in innuendo and slowly driving her crazy wondering if it was innuendo or her conscience distorting his meaning?

Why didn't she just unburden herself and risk his wrath, even perhaps his emotional estrangement, once he knew that the honesty and trust he adhered to was nothing but lip service on her part?

"Wet your lips," he was saying. "A little more to the right. Good, now lift your chin and give me that saucy look."

"Uh . . . Sol?"

"Yes, love?"

Love. He kept calling her that, when more than anything she wanted to hear him say "I love you." Of course, if he said it now, he'd be saying it to a fake. And he'd made it clear he had no use for anything artificial, not even an eyeball, and surely not a wife. But if he'd just say it, she knew she'd feel safe enough to throw herself on his mercy.

Mariah wavered, pitted between what was right and the possible consequences of her wrongdoing. She searched his expectant and open gaze, one that said he trusted her and was patiently waiting for whatever she might have to say. For a moment, she actually thought she could do it.

"Something on your mind?" he prompted.

"Yes. Yes, there is." She tried to force the words, but try as she might, they wouldn't come. A heavy sense of failure and self-disappointment weighed on her. As well as a disturbing remembrance. "Last

Sunday, at the church picnic, when you were roasting the corn, I went for a little walk around the town square. I met an old friend of yours there. Does the name Desiree strike a bell?"

"Desiree?" Sol was suddenly busy with his camera. "Why didn't you tell me you met her?"

"Because . . . well, I got the impression the two of you were very close at one time. I wanted to get over my jealousy before I brought her up so I wouldn't say anything petty or immature. Such as mentioning that she was more undressed than dressed and I didn't care for the way she fawned over you and asked me if you were still as good a lover as she remembered."

Sol uttered a few expletives, then pinned her with a dark look. "Desiree is a troublemaker, Mariah. I slept with her, as I'm sure she took great pleasure in telling you." He paused, which bothered her. "Stay away from Desiree, do you hear me?"

He was wearing that same formidable expression, using that same harsh voice of unbending authority that conjured up nightmares of what she'd have to endure once she made her confession. But apparently, Sol had a few secrets of his own. Secrets about a woman he'd known all his life, a woman she'd be hard pressed to compete with if she weren't married to him—or if their marriage suffered a fatal blow. That fence post might have ample support, but their marriage was still so new she was terrified to test its strength.

"She's beautiful." Mariah sniffed with distaste. There had been a hardness about Desiree, a calculated kind of display of her too-sensual features. "Not only that," Mariah added, "but I'd be a fool not to see that she's still sweet on you."

"Sweet? Desiree's sweet only when it serves her purpose. I'm telling you, Mariah, she'll make waves between us if she can. Desiree is history, and unless you want to do some story-swapping on old lovers and past lives, I'd suggest we drop this topic for another time."

Mariah picked up on his challenge. She was also knocked flat by the sensitive nerve she'd unexpectedly hit; the force of his reaction intensified her old insecurities.

As he stared at her and she stared back, the air pulsed with tension. No, she decided, any confessions that either might make could definitely wait.

"Okay, consider the topic dropped. You don't want me to pry, and I won't. When you're ready you can tell me, of your own free will."

"Fair enough." Sol sighed heavily and shook his head with something close to disgust. "As usual, we seem to think alike, even about the darnedest things. Now let's take the picture. Ma's waiting for you to can pickles and I've got to help Dad vaccinate cows."

Remembering Desiree's voluptuous curves and her hip-swaying saunter, Mariah pressed her arms against her breasts and revealed some cleavage. Deciding that wasn't provocative enough, she leaned vampishly against the barn gate. Besse nuzzled her through the fence.

"Be sure to get Besse too," she said.

"You and that damn cow," he muttered. She replied with a sexy pout and more exposed cleavage.

Sol took one shot, then put aside the camera and studied her—endlessly, it seemed. His lips were tight and his brow creased in disapproval.

"Nice pose," he said shortly.

"You didn't like it?" Well, she thought with a huff, he'd certainly liked Desiree's slutty charms well enough.

"What I like is the real you, and that's not it."

"What makes you so sure?" she challenged, feeling the sting to her feminine ego. "People have different sides to their personalities, even their tastes. Don't underestimate mine, as I apparently did yours." Mariah gave him her back and fed a handful of hay to Besse. "Mom's waiting, so I'd better go on."

Feeling quite smug, she patted Besse's head and turned, intending to brush past him.

Mariah collided with his massive chest instead, and his lips came down on hers, exerting an over-bearing demand. She pushed against him, angry not only for thwarting her exit but for rejecting in her what he'd enjoyed in Desiree.

Sol's mouth was relentless in its plundering and his hands were totally unprincipled in what they grasped. But as their battle of wills ensued, principles ceased to matter to her and she gave up fighting him to return his hungry kisses and heated strokes.

Once she'd succumbed, Sol released her and she grabbed blindly for the gate to keep her balance.

He was ten feet away when he swung his crutches around and pointed a stern finger in her direction.

"Mariah," he said in a rough, warning tone. "*Be careful.*"

"Let's see, honey. The vinegar mixture is made and heating up—"

"To approximately two hundred and twenty degrees, right?"

"Well . . . I suppose. Just a hard boil, my mother taught me. I'm not sure of the exact degrees."

"Two-twenty," Mariah said absentmindedly. She cleaned another cucumber and tossed it in with the others in a heap. "Remove the blossoms from an unwaxed variety," she muttered to herself. So caught up in the adventure of canning, she was barely aware of LaVerne's curious eavesdropping as she recited the instructions she'd memorized from just a quick glance through the recipe book.

"Use granulated pickling and high-grade vinegar of four to six percent acid. No copper, brass, galvanized, or iron utensils. Stoneware, aluminum, glass, stainless steel advised. Bread and butter. Dill. Sweet gherkin. Quick mustard . . ."

"I'm finished," Mariah called out. "Thanks for letting me help, Mom. This is a total blast."

"Well, it's certainly . . . interesting," LaVerne answered from mere inches behind her.

Mariah jumped. "Oh, I—I thought you were by the stove."

"No. Just getting a lesson on pickling, when I thought *I* was teacher for the day. Didn't you tell me you'd never even eaten a homemade pickle, honey?"

"I—well, I—" Mariah stared helplessly at the cucumbers. "It's really simple. I just—"

"Mariah." LaVerne's voice was softly chiding. "Why don't you tell me the truth? Even a blind person could see you're hiding something."

Tears burned behind Mariah's tightly squeezed lids. Cornered without warning. *What was she going to do?*

"Come sit with me, honey." LaVerne urged her to the sunny breakfast nook. Taking a seat opposite her, she reached for Mariah's hands, which were folded in earnest prayer, and pressed them between hers.

"Mariah, you're obviously a very bright young lady—bright enough, I hope, to realize you can't run and hide forever. Being a parent, I can't help but wonder if yours are missing you. It's not right to worry them."

"They're not missing me." Taking a steadying

breath, she plunged ahead. "At least not yet. They're still in Europe."

"They don't know you're married to my son, do they?"

"Not . . . exactly." Glancing out the window, Mariah saw Sol heading toward the house. Anxiety clutched at her stomach. "Sol's coming, Mom. Please, don't tell him—"

"That's your place, not mine," LaVerne assured her. "But I would like to know why you hid the truth from your folks, then took off once their backs were turned. Was it a bad home, Mariah? Were you mistreated?"

"Not mistreated. Just . . . misunderstood. I was unhappy and so I took it upon myself to change that. I regret the way I went about it, but I don't regret anything else. Sol's a wonderful man," she said passionately. "I didn't know how to stand up to my parents to tell them that before, but when they get back, I swear I will."

LaVerne smiled as she looked out the window at her son. "Judging from the way you stand up to that ornery boy of mine, I imagine you will. He's given you some practice at it, hasn't he?"

"Daily doses." Deciding LaVerne was an ally, Mariah risked a burning question. "He gave me a dose of something I wasn't expecting today. It was about Desiree."

LaVerne jerked her attention from the window. She had the look of a bantam hen protecting its young.

"What about that girl?"

"I met her, and she was no girl. She was—"

"A floozy. A spoiled-rotten, rich snob without a stitch of moral fiber who practically got my son down the aisle."

Mariah could feel the blood drain from her face. "You mean Sol . . . and Desiree were engaged?"

"If he didn't tell you, honey, then it's not my place to do the tattling."

Tapping a finger on the table, LaVerne said firmly, "You didn't ask for my advice, but this once I'm giving it anyway. Your marriage is new and I understand a need for time before heaping some manure on the perfume of love. But what you and Sol have is good. Don't take too long before you trust it; otherwise one cow patty gets tossed on top of another and before you know it you've got a whole heap of dung to deal with. Don't let it pile up."

The front door banged open and both women jumped as if caught in a conspiracy. They scooted out of the nook.

"Thanks, Mom." Giving her a quick hug, Mariah said softly, "I've always heard you don't just marry one person, you marry a whole family. I lucked out both ways."

"Works 'both ways' all right, Mariah." LaVerne heartily patted her back. "You're good for my son, and I thank God every day that he's married to you and not that *Desiree*." She all but spat the name out, much to Mariah's satisfaction. "Just one more question. How did you come upon so much know-how in the pickle department?"

"I guess you could say it has a lot to do with why I'm here and why my parents don't know it."

"Yo, what's this?" Sol's frame filled the kitchen doorway. The memory of his warning kiss arced between him and Mariah, as did her stung pride. It wasn't a comfortable feeling, especially with the secrets between her and LaVerne.

When Mariah stepped back, LaVerne put a protective arm about her, then wrinkled a nose at her son.

"Well, Sol, did you come in here to stare at us while

looking like you just downed a quart of those sour pickles on the boil, or have you got news?"

"Besse's acting like she's ready to have that calf," he said flatly. "I thought Mariah would like to know."

"She's calving!" Mariah darted for the door, but stopped short. "Oh, the pickles. Mom—"

"Go on. You know enough about pickling to set up your own cannery, so shoo. Go keep Besse company."

Mariah stared up at Sol. She was still irked at him, but he had come to tell her about Besse. Deciding he deserved a peck on the cheek, she kissed him and took off.

When Sol turned to follow her, LaVerne snapped out, "You just wait one good minute, young man. What's the meaning of stomping into my kitchen and glaring at your wife like that?"

"That's mine and Mariah's business, Ma. I'd thank you to keep your nose out of it."

"Just so you keep yours clean."

"And what do you mean by that?"

"Think about it, son. And while you've got your brain kicked into gear, remember one thing: A man usually treats his wife the way he's seen his father treat his mother. The next time you come in here to fetch your wife, take a few pointers from your daddy and don't come empty-handed."

It never ceased to amaze him that no matter how old a man got, he could still feel like a kid called on the carpet with one sharp word from his mother.

"What did you expect me to do, Ma, bring her flowers?"

"Good idea, son. It takes half a minute to yank a fistful of posies out of the yard. And don't you dare go back to that barn without some from my garden—to go along with a kiss for your wife for putting up with my prodigal son."

Eleven

"She might be at this awhile, Mariah. Dinner's already cold, so why don't we go ahead and eat, then check back on Besse in an hour or so?"

"But she could have the calf while we're gone." Stroking the long-suffering cow, who was bearing up stoically, Mariah glanced at Sol. His attitude had improved considerably since he'd returned to the barn, flowers in hand, several hours before. "Everyone else left once the last milking was done and I don't want her to be on her own."

"For heaven's sake, it's not as if you won't get another chance to see a calf born. They get dropped around here like flies."

"But they're not Besse's. She's special, and I'm not about to leave her in her time of need."

"'Her time of need'? She's just a cow," Sol insisted.

"Don't you listen to him, Besse," Mariah said, covering the cow's ears. Besse rolled her eyes to the side. "He's just jealous because you won't pay him any attention."

"If I'm jealous, it's because you're giving her more

attention than you are me." When he nudged her behind with a crutch, Mariah spun around to see him quirk a brow and give a half smile.

In his own way he was trying to make up, she realized. LaVerne had probably given him the idea for the flowers, but stroking her with his crutch was typically Sol. Whether he was infuriating or gruffly sweet, she did find him irresistible—even when she didn't want to.

Looping her arms around his neck, she pressed her cheek against his chest. He embraced her, and she felt his heart thudding out a steady, reassuring beat. Moments like this, when she felt such completion, made her heart ache.

"I'm sorry we had words today," she said quietly. "I can't stand any distance between us." She hated her cowardice, the insecurities that created the invisible chasm he couldn't know was there.

"Neither can I, love." He held her tighter. "But it's up to us to close any distance that exists."

Mariah searched for a hidden meaning to his words, but his expression was unreadable. So she took him at face value and nodded.

"Marriage isn't easy, is it, Sol?"

"They say the first year's the hardest. We're still feeling our way around, and in some ways it's like the blind leading the blind. We'll get through it. It's just a matter of paying our dues. Nothing worth having is for free."

And having Sol meant paying up; the price could be his distrust, his distance, the end of the marriage. Digging her toes into the hay, she sighed wistfully.

"I know it's wrong to wish your life away, but sometimes, Sol, I can't help but wish we had this first year behind us."

"What? And miss out on all the discoveries yet to

come?" He lifted her chin, and his smile was bitter-sweet. "Just think of all the moments like this we'll have to share. Even arguments have their purpose in the weaving of a marriage."

"Arguing is the pits," she interjected. "And it's one part of the tapestry I wish we could leave out."

"No such thing, Mariah. This might be my first and only marriage, but I saw enough head-butting growing up to know there's no getting around it." He raised a brow. "Didn't you ever see your parents have one doozy of a row?"

"No. Any disagreements they ever had they kept to themselves. But I wish—" What she wished was that she *had* seen them have a few good brouhahas. If she had, maybe she'd know how to handle conflict and resolution, instead of floundering around in all these murky unknowns. Projection. Rationalization. Denial. She knew she was guilty of all those things, but what it came down to was guts, and that was something she was going to have to find on her own.

"You wish . . . what?"

"Right now I wish they'd been a little less fond of each other and butted heads more often in front of me. Then maybe I could deal better with paying certain dues."

"Is that a fact?" Sol shook his head. "It's a pity you never saw them fight, Mariah. That's quite an education you missed out on. Watching Ma and Dad, I learned there's a real art to clearing the air and putting things right."

Mariah looked at him curiously. Whether or not he was alluding to more than the obvious, she didn't know, but she was eager to have any insights he could provide.

"And just what exactly is the right way to go about settling your differences?"

"First, you have to have some ground rules. No name-calling; that's a biggie. Door-slamming . . . That's kind of iffy, and so is stomping around. It might let off some steam, but all that noise tends to rile things up a bit more."

"You mean it adds some spice to what's already simmering on the back burner?"

"I'll say—like cayenne pepper. Of course, the silent treatment is almost worse than too much racket. When one won't talk back, the other person usually starts talking too much. That's when things really start brewing, and it's like the lull before the storm. Anybody around better take cover because things could start flying soon."

Mariah combed her memory for an experience she could relate this to. She'd never had to take cover at her house. A vision of pots and pans sailing through the air and vases smashed on the floor had her gaping.

"But throwing things—that's immature. Uncivilized."

"You're right. That's why throwing things and hitting is absolutely not allowed. What I mean is, *words* start to fly. And this is the tricky part, something that takes a lot of skill—sticking to the subject at hand. Tempting as it is, you can't dredge up old garbage. And saying things like, hmmm, let's see . . ."

Putting a hand on his hip, he spoke in a falsetto. "I'm sick and tired of picking up your dirty, smelly socks, and if you track manure onto my clean floor one more time I'm going to rub your nose in it. And don't you know what deodorant is? I can smell you from here. Now go take a shower and just leave me alone." Sol chuckled when Mariah giggled at his imitation of LaVerne. "Of course, socks and floors and deodorant don't have a dang thing to do with the real issue. That's just the lead-in."

"Now let me guess at the comeback." Fully into the spirit of the conversation, Mariah tightened her lips the way she'd seen Herbert do, a mannerism he'd apparently passed on to his son. "'I'll take a shower when I'm damn good and ready. Or better yet when you quit dumping too much salt into the chicken noodle soup.'"

"Vegetable beef," Sol corrected. "You've got it, baby. But once all that nonsense is past, it's time to get to the meat of the matter. Kinda like foreplay before making love. Oh, that's another thing—never go to bed mad. And *never* bring up the tacky present you hated but didn't say anything about."

Making mental notations for any future confrontation, Mariah said, "Okay, no slurs on—"

"In-laws. *Especially* in-laws."

"Gifts, in-laws: taboo. Check. So then what?"

"Then someone—whoever feels he or she has been wronged—has to take the first bite. Just a nip to begin with usually—to test the waters, so to speak, to find out what's going to hit home and what's going to go *splat*."

"But what if it's something really important? Something that could have far-reaching effects?"

Sol was quiet for a moment. "That's different. One of those matters that people who love each other have to discuss at length behind closed doors. No one can solve something difficult overnight. I think that's where trust and loyalty and commitment come in. But nothing's insurmountable, Mariah. Not when two people really care."

Sol cared. She cared . . . too much. Afraid he would see her internal struggle, she looked down.

"And how do the little issues finally get resolved?"

"The same way the big ones should. Like this." He pressed his palm to her chin, his fingertips spreading on either side of her jaw, then lifted her face and demanded a straight gaze. The brush of his lips against hers followed. "The best part of all, Mariah. Kiss and make up."

The kiss they shared was hot and sweet, everything any woman could possibly want. His embrace was urgent and gentle, sweeping her away from the ceaseless gnaw of worry and doubt.

"Happy?" His evening beard grazed her head, prickling her scalp and sending a ripple of gooseflesh down her arms.

Was she happy? No—she was ecstatic. And miserable. *Trust. Loyalty.* How they haunted her, kept her awake even when his lessening pain allowed him to sleep. LaVerne was right: Borrowed time was one thing, but like milk, it could sour if left on the shelf too long.

Three weeks and no more, she vowed. Three weeks to come to terms with herself, find her guts, then take on one of those arguments with Sol, and expose all. *She* would be exposed, stripped of all pretense and pride, because there was nothing to be proud about in perpetuating deceit, even for the best of reasons.

Content with her decision, but less than ever with herself, Mariah relished the moment. She relished life, and she relished this complex man.

"Am I happy?" she said. "Right now, I'm happier than I've ever been in my life. And that's the truth."

"Me too." He rubbed his chin against her hair. "By the way, happy anniversary. Five weeks and two days since I got off that plane and you told me to get my crutch myself."

Mariah chuckled. "I wasn't very gracious about it."

"Thank God. I have to say that incident made me realize that marrying you was the smartest thing I'd ever done in my life. I shudder every time I remember telling Turns that if I had it to do over again I wouldn't repeat my vows."

The laughter died in her throat. "You told him that?"

"I was recuperating, Mariah, and feeling pretty bad about life in general. I didn't want to drag you down with me. Turns was quick to point out that he hoped you gave me a reason to get back on my feet—to run in the opposite direction, if nothing else."

"I should send Turns a thank-you note, I guess. That's a left-handed compliment if I ever heard one."

Sol ruffled her hair and laughed. "He's a smart bastard, all right. But if that marriage certificate doesn't show in the mail soon, I'm going to light into him like a lit stick of dynamite."

Her birth certificate! How could she have forgotten, even if she had been lulled into feeling that nothing could touch her here, that she was protected from reality by the security of "home, sweet home." Sol *had* to know before she sent it. Suddenly, three weeks seemed as unrealistic as a year.

"Did, um . . ." Mariah nervously wet her lips. "Did Turns say what was holding things up?"

Sol eyed her curiously. "Yeah. The certificate has to go through certain channels with the government so you're recognized as my wife and can share my benefits. Just a formality, and I know the government can be slow, but this is ridiculous. In fact, I'll give him a call tomorrow and find out what's going on."

"No!" Mariah managed a convincing smile while dealing with the urge to throw up. "I mean really,

Sol, he's a trusted friend. I'm sure he's taking care of everything as fast as he can. Wait a few more weeks. It's probably already in the mail."

How could she have been so shortsighted, frittering away the days as if paradise had no end? Five weeks of nirvana and a crash course in solving marital problems was all she had, except for a husband who invoked *trust* and *honesty* like a litany and—*Oh God, please, just a little more time before the walls come tumbling down and bury her underneath.*

"You and I both know letters can get lost in the mail," Mariah said quickly. *Calm, stay calm,* she frantically ordered herself. "I remember one that took a month to reach me."

"I still have all the ones you sent me. Sometimes I reread them." Sol fanned his face. "Whew, baby. Some of those things are scorchers. I'm surprised they didn't ignite in transit."

Heaving an inner sigh of relief that she'd apparently changed his mind about calling Turns immediately, Mariah allowed herself a shaky laugh.

"How about I go round up dinner?" Sol reached past her and gave Besse a pat. "I'll bring it back to the barn and we can have a picnic. Sound good?"

The fluorescent glow of the barn light blended with the shaft of moonlight piercing through the far rafters and reflected off his gold wedding band. Mariah laid her hand over his, and their rings met. This was hers; Sol was hers. A knot of determination took hold. *Two* weeks, no more.

"Think you could smuggle in a bottle of wine?" she suggested with a lightness she didn't feel.

"Maybe I'll bring two. An extra one to share once Besse has that calf so we can sleep in our bed instead of a pile of hay." With a quick, parting kiss,

Sol turned to go, then stopped. "About Desiree . . . she means nothing to me, Mariah. Less than nothing. You mean everything she could never be."

"But she meant a lot to you at one time, didn't she?"

"I thought she did. But I was in lust, not in love. Actually, it took some miles between Desiree and me for me to put her in her proper perspective."

"And what is Desiree's proper perspective?"

"That's a complicated answer. We went through a lot together when we were much younger. After my last visit, though, something happened that got her out of my system for good. But . . . we'll talk about it another time." His smile didn't reach his eye. "We have an anniversary to celebrate."

Remembering her vow not to pry, and unsure if she was equipped to handle Sol's past when she was struggling with her own, Mariah touched his cheek. She felt empathy with whatever pain Desiree had brought him. But it also frightened her, because if Desiree had been capable of hurting him once, she might still have access to his heart.

"I know what it's like to want to forget things that won't go away, no matter how hard you try to pretend they don't exist." At least they could connect in this, and any connection they had strengthened their bonds.

"Yes, Mariah," he said softly, "I imagine that you, more than anyone, do."

Twelve

As Sol exited the barn, Mariah's cooing to Besse wisped through his ears and touched a gentle chord deep inside him.

Where Desiree was conniving and self-centered, Mariah was caring and good and compassionate, qualities she extended even to a dumb cow—and to a sometimes even dumber husband, one dumb enough to have almost married the wrong woman.

As he neared the house, an uneasy sensation stitched through his vitals. His sweet wife had actually come face-to-face with Desiree, the black widow spider that could have killed him in bed any number of times; a woman he'd known since childhood, to whom he'd be married now if she hadn't so cold-heartedly erased his only reason for proposing less than two years ago.

He hadn't seen Desiree since he'd returned, but she was due a visit and a warning. The woman wouldn't think twice about getting back at him by boasting to Mariah about their short-term engagement and slanting the facts.

Sol muttered a vile word. The thought of touching Desiree again left him cold, after the ecstasy of holding Mariah. What he and Mariah had was almost too good—except for her continued silence, which was as much his fault as hers. But one direct accusation and she'd fold like a matchstick house hit by a gust of wind. He wanted her to confess of her volition—a sign of the trust he'd been doing his damnedest to earn and to convey she could rely on.

The cattle run came into his view—two parallel bars with enough space between them to pin a cow . . . *or to accommodate him.*

As he contemplated it, his mind drew a picture: Mariah flipping through a book on the porch swing. Her attention suddenly drawn away as he ran up the steps and threw his crutches at her feet. The wooden planks solid beneath him as he picked her up and carried her, amazed and crying, over the threshold.

Sol set his crutches aside. His private, strenuous workouts had resulted in physical anguish and an encouraging amount of progress. Now was as good a time as any to test himself.

After assuring himself the area was deserted, he stood in the cattle run and held on to the bars. He looked straight ahead, but rather than seeing the impossible distance to the end of the run, he saw The Vision through the camera of his mind.

Sol released the bars, his palms hovering over the metal. Holding his breath, he willed his right leg to take a single step. He teetered, but refused the ready help of the bars. Next came the left foot. The few inches were a slow, agonizing journey, and only sheer will got him through.

"Did it," he whispered triumphantly. "Now take another. . . . That's it, another. . . . Walk to Mariah. You can do—aghh!" Sol nearly bit off his tongue to keep from screaming. His knees were bent almost to the ground, but he held his weight up by clutching the bars.

The sweat bathing his brow had cooled by the time he reached the farmhouse. Twenty minutes later, he was gripping a picnic basket.

Sol bid his parents good night, feeling an unmistakable satisfaction in being home, looking forward to the romantic night ahead with his wife, and still feeling pride over his earlier accomplishment. From here on, he and the cattle run had a daily date of an hour in the dark.

His gaze was fixed on the muted light seeping from the open barn door when he heard a high-pitched wail. Stopping dead in his tracks, he waited on edge, then heard it again.

"*Mariah!*" Sol dropped the picnic basket and took off across the seemingly endless yard. He almost fell on his face as his instincts rushed ahead of his body. *God, how he hated this.* Cursing his legs, he heard his wife screaming, screaming.

And he couldn't run.

The night became a full-moon howl. Mariah's wretched sobs laced with the eerie tendrils of black clouds obscuring the pale moonlight. A whistling wind seemed to taunt his ears as his racing heart pounded to the beat of his crutches striking the ground. Sol was filled with a sense of unreality, as if he were in a slow-motion ride that suddenly speeded up, when he caught sight of the horrific scene in the barn.

"Mariah! Mariah, what—oh, dear God . . ." He went to her, his vision locked on the blood-streaked arm that was stretched out to him. Blood dripped through her fingers.

"S-Sol." She got up from Besse's stall and half

wove, half stumbled toward him while he hurried to catch her in his arms. "Besse . . . Besse's dead."

Unable to take his gaze off her blood-soaked blouse and the red-streaked hand tearing at his shirt, he gripped her arms firmly and assured himself she was still whole.

"You're covered with blood," he said with a harshness born of panic. "Why the hell are you covered with blood?"

"Besse's dead . . . Besse's dead," she chanted. Sol shook her until she fell silent and merely stared at him.

"Okay, baby, Besse's dead. Now, please, just tell me why this blood is all over you."

"Prolapsed uterus ruptured . . . hemorrhaging . . . ovarian vessels . . . must be internal bleeding too . . . then Besse's down. Finally my arm's inside, have to find the vessel and pinch it, but it's too late, the blood won't stop . . . ruptured uterus and Besse's dead . . . Besse's—"

Her voice broke and she wept with the tears of the bereaved. Sol gathered her to him and rocked her against his chest, stroked his fingers through her hair while he murmured words and sounds of comfort.

After she'd cried so long her sobs were reduced to dry heaves and then silence, Sol held her away. His voice was kind, but firm.

"I'm sorry, Mariah, because I know you loved Besse. But this is a farm, and animals dying is a fact of life. You have no choice but to accept that. You have to accept it now."

Her nod was jerky, and his heart gave a lurch when she stoically lifted her trembling chin. She impatiently scrubbed her cheeks and wiped her nose against her arm, smearing the blood over her face, like lipstick. He tried to rub it off, but she shoved his hand away.

Her eyes shone with understanding, with a maturity that came from hardening oneself against a devastating blow. And a touch of humiliation for such abject loss of control, which he derisively attributed to her proper upbringing.

"You're right, of course," she said in a raw voice. "How silly of me. Why, it's ridiculous, isn't it, falling to—to pieces over a dumb cow?"

"She wasn't a dumb cow to you, and I'd thank you never to be embarrassed in front of me for exposing any strong emotion. I know how you feel—the same way I felt when I was a kid and saw my dog get hit by a car. Cried every night for a month. It tore me up so bad I swore I'd never own another one."

"Sounds like good advice, Sol. No more pets for me, not after this. Excuse me, I—"

"Wait." He stilled her with an iron-tight grip. "Your feelings could change. Mine did. Three months after Raja died, a stray decided to adopt me. I ended up calling him Dog because I didn't want to get too attached. Funny thing about Dog, I got attached anyway."

Mariah studied her bloodstained blouse, examined her crimson hand as if it weren't a part of her. "The calf lived," she said distantly. "I guess you should check on it. I need to wash myself."

"Is it cute?"

She shrugged. "I don't know and I don't care. It got up on its legs just before Besse fell on hers."

"You shouldn't blame the calf for Besse's death."

"I blame myself, not the calf," she snapped, glaring at him. "If I'd run to call the vet instead of trying to save her myself, she might be alive right now." Her lips were pinched as she whispered, "'Meant to be a surgeon.' What a crock of—"

"Who's meant to be a surgeon—you?"

"*Never*," she said flatly, and spun on her heel.

"Mariah, stop." She did, but didn't turn to face him. "You actually performed a lifesaving technique on Besse?" She nodded curtly, and he saw her fist clench, the dried blood on it verifying what he could hardly believe. "You did the right thing. The vet never would have made it in time. You gave her a chance, and you're wrong not to give yourself one too." No comment. He sighed heavily, then said, "When you're through washing up, I could use your help."

Sol watched her stiff retreat. She went to the far end of the barn and mechanically began to soap her arms at the washbasin. She could have passed for a surgeon cleaning up after a machine-gun party. Another piece to fit into the puzzle of Mariah.

With a perplexed shake of his head, Sol went to the pen.

"Lord," he groaned. Besse was lying in her own blood; the tinny smell filled his nostrils. In his mind he saw Mariah performing the crude procedure, then hugging her dead cow, heedless of the foul matter beneath her. His anger was swift—anger at himself for not being there, and at Mariah for blaming herself for a tragedy she'd done her damnedest to avert yet believed herself responsible for.

Her reaction told him a lot, and it disturbed him deeply. The Marines had taught him plenty about training people until they fit into a certain mold. Mariah had been conditioned to perform, and failure wasn't an option. Neither was a healthy venting of emotion. It was twisted, unhealthy, and he was sure it all came compliments of her uppity parents. They were almost certain to try to take their daughter back. *Just let 'em try.*

His disgusted snort coincided with a tiny, pitiful *mooo.*

"You poor little dogie," he said to the calf. "Mariah can't miss your mama half as much as you're going to."

Unlike many dairy farmers, the Standishes didn't immediately separate calves from their mothers to nurse a bottle, choosing instead to let nature take its course. Not necessarily sensible, but in his mind, right.

A slow smile tugged at his lips. No need for Mariah to know that the calf didn't need Besse to survive just fine.

The calf stared myopically at Sol with big brown eyes, then looked down at its deceased mother before nudging her with a little black nose. All wobbly legs and matted hair, since Besse hadn't been alive to clean it up.

Leaning his crutches against the stall, Sol got down painfully on his knees and examined the calf's head. A fine specimen, thanks to a breeding catalogue and artificial insemination.

"You about done, Mariah?" Sol called, deciding the best thing he could do was to put her to work.

"Yes," she said behind him.

"Got you a job, baby. You clean up the orphan while I do what I can with this mess."

"I'll take care of Besse," she said adamantly.

"Besse's gone, love. If you really want to do something for her, you'll see to her youngun. I'm afraid I can't pick it up and . . ." He raised the tail and determined the gender. "It's a heifer. She doesn't want to leave. Go get a rope, okay?"

"I'll get Dad. He can help."

"Everyone's asleep by now since milking time comes early. We'll see to this by ourselves." When she didn't move, he reverted to the tone he'd used to say "Frog!" and make his men jump without asking how high.

"C'mon, woman, get your butt in gear. We've got a job to do. Crying time's over, so go get that rope, unless you want to nurse this baby yourself. The calf needs cleaning and some milk. Both of those chores go to you."

Sol caught a foul word from his usually proper wife, who seemed to have assimilated more from him than just the techniques of dairy farming. He was still grinning when she practically knocked him in the head with the twine.

"There's the rope. Tie it up and I'll pull."

"Sounds like a deal." Sol looped a noose around the calf's neck and silently asked its forgiveness for what he needed to do. Cinching it tight, he threw the end to Mariah, then slapped the calf's backside. "Get outta here, you runt!"

"Sol!" The calf trotted toward Mariah when she gently tugged the rope. "You're hurting it."

"Since when do you care?" he said, then slapped its flanks once more when it stalled.

"You don't have to mistreat the poor thing," she yelled. "It's just a baby." Stooping to stroke the matted hair as it *mooo*ed against her neck, she shot Sol a censuring glare.

"It's a dogie, Mariah. It doesn't have a mama and we'll be lucky to find a willing substitute. It could die of starvation if the other cows reject it. Then who's going to feed it? A bottle takes time, and I don't have it to give."

"*I'll* feed it a bottle," she retorted hotly. "Now go about your business, since you obviously don't care one way or the other. I've got some cleaning to do and so do you."

Mariah whispered something into the calf's ear while it looked at her as if she could be trusted.

"Oh, Mariah," he said offhandedly when it affectionately nudged her legs. "Got a name picked out yet?"

She looked from him to Besse to the dogie.

"Cow," she said, swiping at her eyes.

Sol laughed silently.

Thirteen

"Got that calf fed yet, Mariah? It's already two and we need to get to town and back before milking time."

"Almost done, Sol," she yelled back as the ten-day-old calf emptied the bottle. "Hurry up, Cow," she whispered. "Beth's waiting for me to call." Thank God for the library and the nearby pay phone, since privacy was scarce at their cottage. Though this would be her last clandestine check-in.

"Want me to drop you at the library?"

Mariah jerked at the unexpected closeness of Sol's voice. There was a terseness in his tone that caused her to yank the bottle from the calf, which promptly sounded its dismay.

"That would be great," she said, getting to her feet and risking a glance at his unsmiling face.

"What are you reading up on this time . . . baby?"

His odd emphasis on the endearment prickled the fine hair on her neck.

"A name-your-baby book. I decided that Cow

needs a proper name. Names are very important, you know. They stick for life."

"And a few come to mind right now that I could apply to *you*." His lips twisted strangely, and he looked at her strangely too. Mariah held her breath so long her lungs began to burn. But then he quirked a brow and smiled devilishly.

"Names like Sweet Heat, Hot Mama, and, of course, *love*. Now give me a hug before we head for town. Be a good girl and I'll buy you a frozen custard, and maybe even that antique rocker you've set your heart on."

She hugged him, all right—hugged him to keep from slumping to the barn floor. She must be paranoid. Sol would never toy with her, would he? Make her think he was about to break a ground rule and call her a yellow-bellied coward and a sneaky little cheat, then once he'd made her squirm, heap on some affection. He'd never be that devious, would he?

No. No, she was the devious one, not him. She had to be projecting her anxieties onto Sol, that was all.

Cow nuzzled her jean-clad leg and Mariah was grateful for the comfort. At least she had told a bit of truth—by the time she returned she'd have a name picked out for her little dogie.

Sol pulled into the library parking lot and cut the truck's engine. Mariah hesitated before she reached for the door handle.

"You're going to wait this time?" she asked. "But I thought you had some errands to run."

"They shouldn't take long, and neither should checking out a name-your-baby book." He reached over and pulled the handle that she seemed so close to strangling. "Hop out. I'm coming along."

Sol smiled grimly when she darted a furtive, frantic glance at the nearby pay phone. Yep, she was anxious all right. Mad as he was, he was going to enjoy stretching her anxiety until she snapped and the lid blew.

Calculating his next move, he stayed on her heels as they went through the library. While she checked out a book of names, he decided that Mariah was damn lucky she'd chosen today to name her cow, what with the state he was in. He'd gone to the barn to confront her about a very disturbing bit of news he'd received over the phone. But at the sight of her and Cow and her announcement about the name, he'd known the confrontation would have to wait. If it weren't for that tragic night and her just getting over it, he'd probably still be shaking her like a dog just out of a tick bath.

"Second stop, frozen custard," Sol said. They emerged from the library and Mariah glanced around nervously. "Why don't we walk?" he said. "It's only a block away and the weather's beautiful— for now. Don't you agree, *love*?"

"Uh, yes—no. What did you just say?"

"After the frozen custard we'll go to the antique store. I think my lovely, sweet, darling wife deserves that rocker for a special occasion." Laying it on so thick he was ready to gag, Sol continued, "Six weeks and five days since you threw down my crutch and knocked me off my feet." *A crutch I'd like to take to your butt, little lady.*

"Really, Sol, you don't have to do that. It's too much and, besides, I can wait."

"I can't," he muttered. Then, remembering he wanted to butter her up so much that she'd slip when he dropped the bomb, Sol forced a smile and graciously waved her up to the frozen-custard stand.

After insisting she get a triple hot fudge custard boat with sprinkles—"Only the best for my beautiful bride"—he led her to an outside table, making sure the pay phone was in sight.

He downed his own cone quickly, then dabbed away the rich confection beside Mariah's mouth.

"I need to make a short stop at the County Records Office for some *paperwork* on the farm. A few *documents* Ma asked me to check on. Want to come along?"

"That's okay," she said eagerly. "You go ahead and I'll just enjoy the breeze." All chatty now, she went on, "Why, can you believe it's sweltering in Mobile right now, and here we sit eating ice cream that's not even melting?"

"It's cool today, babe, but things could heat up pretty quick."

When she hit him with a did-you-mean-that-the-way-I-think-you-did expression, he smiled innocently.

"Enjoy yourself while you can." Getting up, he stretched and added, "Yes, sir, the weather's fickle around here. Never can tell if a storm might blow in or when a sudden change could overtake the pleasant climate."

She caught his hand on the crutches.

"Sol . . . I—"

"Yes? Something I need to know before I take off?"

"Will you be gone long?"

Sol swallowed a foul word and shrugged. "Say, twenty minutes. Of course, if you'd rather I wait—"

"No! No, you go on. The sooner you leave, the sooner you'll be back."

And the sooner she could use those quarters he'd heard jangling around in her purse.

Sol left her with a kiss, then set off in the direction opposite from the phone. Half a block down, he ducked behind a building and checked his watch. Five minutes before he backtracked.

He did a few knee bends, hoping to work some of the fury out of his system. He still couldn't believe it. All this time, and he'd just found out the holdup on their marriage certificate wasn't because of the government—it was his *wife!*

Brother, had Turns had some explaining to do. That silent treatment he'd warned Mariah about had the desired effect: Turns had kept talking, stammering, apologizing.

"See, man, it was like this. She said her birth certificate got lost the first time—"

As if she'd actually sent it to begin with, Sol thought with a snarl. She didn't want anyone to know her age, no doubt, but that was no excuse. Mariah was going to grow up and face some facts of life real fast.

"I didn't say anything 'cause you were ranting and raving about wanting out and I—do you still want out? You're sure this marriage is going to work? . . . Okay, sorry, I'll mind my own business. . . . Sure, Sol, sure, I'll be looking for it, get the marriage certificate pronto and put it in the works for the Unit Diary. . . . Yes, yes, they'll back-date it to the day the wedding took place. . . . Yeah, I know you're mad—okay, damn disgusted. . . . No, you don't have to fly over here and chew me up while you walk it through yourself. . . ."

Adrenaline and anger surged through Sol's legs. It blended with The Vision—an image so embedded in his mind he could taste it, see it, feel it. The two mixed and collided and he swore he felt strong as a bull.

Sol glanced around to make sure he was alone. He was either going to take his first step alone or he was going to be kissing concrete.

Straddled between the urge to strangle Mariah and to pick her up in his arms, he set his crutches aside. Pressing a hand against the nearby wall, he willed his right leg a few inches forward. Gritting his teeth, he held his balance, released the wall, and slid his bad leg up. Wobbling, he repeated the movement seven times. Seven steps without a crutch or a bar for support.

"Hot damn!" he whooped in a whispered shout. "Hot damn. Call it the cripple's shuffle, but it's a dance that feels better than the Beer Barrel Polka."

He raised two fists in victory and almost toppled over. After managing a few more steps, he clutched the wall once more. His head hung down while he drew in ragged gulps of air.

Five minutes had passed—five miraculous minutes. His spirits were high and his body was still pumping adrenaline as he latched on to the crutches and took off.

Standing across the street from the custard stand, he didn't see Mariah at any of the tables. But when he peered down the block, he could just make out her figure before she whirled around and hung up the phone.

Probably checking to see if Mommy and Daddy were back. Damn, how could she keep anything from him after all they'd shared? He'd given her more than ample time to come clean, even a few pointers on how to do it.

Once she named her calf, the first domino was

going down, and he couldn't wait to watch them all fall.

Hiding behind a tree, Sol could almost hear the slap of her tennis shoes on the sidewalk as she quickly made her way to the stand. Several minutes after she'd seated herself at a table, he approached. She stretched as if she'd been warming her buns the entire time. The urge to warm them up with his palm was real tempting.

"Back so soon?" she chirped, grabbing her purse, which had ceased to jingle.

"Let's head for the truck and pick up the rocker. Looks like we're in for some thunder and lightning."

Book in hand, Mariah looked to the sky as she hurried to keep up with him.

"Are you sure? Everything looks clear to me."

"Not to me, babe." He wet a fingertip and held it in the air between them. "Yep, my inner barometer says there's a storm on the horizon."

"If you say so," she said breathlessly.

"I say so. Decide on a name for your calf?"

"Hilda," she said. They reached the truck, and as Mariah got in, Sol leveled her with a meaningful one-eyed glare. Then he twined a hand in her hair and yanked her for a mouth-to-mouth assault. He administered an angry kiss, one she likely took for passion. Once he was done and she was gasping, making sure no one had seen, he slammed her door, got into the driver's seat, and peeled out.

After they had driven in silence for a few minutes, Mariah said uncertainly, "I decided to name her Hilda because it means 'battle maid.' She lost Besse when I did, and it's been a struggle ever since for Cow—Hilda—to buck the odds. She's strong, but she's still fighting a tough war. No one really wanted to take her in but me, and sometimes I worry that no matter how much I care, how hard I try to see to her needs, it's just not enough. Do you think I picked the right name?"

"Apt handle," he said with conviction. "Trust me."

The low rumble of thunder rolled prophetically in the distance.

"Talked to Turns yesterday," Sol said nonchalantly.

Mariah looked up from her knitting and was greeted with nothing but the back page of a newspaper and Sol's bare feet propped on an old ottoman.

Mariah resumed knitting Sol's soon-to-be thirty-first-birthday present and glanced uneasily at the phone on the Shaker table between them.

"How was Turns?" she asked uneasily.

"Fine." Sol turned a page. "Except he's run into a problem with our marriage certificate."

"A problem? What kind of a problem?" Mariah's heart turned over, skidded to a halt, then slammed against her ribs at his next words.

"Seems there's a birth certificate that got lost . . . or never showed on his end of the paper jungle. You wouldn't happen to know anything about that, would you . . . *love*?"

The knitting needles stilled. "I—I have no idea what happened. Maybe I should send him another copy."

"'Maybe'?" Sol folded the newspaper into a neat square, then flipped it onto the floor and stabbed her with a glare. "Tomorrow's not soon enough to suit me. Got it handy? I'll make a copy first thing in the morning and get it in the mail to where it should've been weeks ago."

The yarn and needles dropped from Mariah's

numb fingers into her equally numb lap. She was numb all over. Her vision had narrowed to Sol's menacing expression, and her heart speeded up, thudding rat-a-tat-tat before climbing into her throat to raise her voice an octave.

"W-what makes you th-think I didn't s-send it?"

With a snarl, he got to his feet and reached for his crutches. If she hadn't been so terrified of how he was stalking toward her, she might have been amazed to see him move with a new agility. But as it was, he was looming over her, his hands clenching and unclenching, his blue eye glowering down at her. The patch seemed like a death flag.

"Game's up, Mariah," he gritted out. "My patience has run out, and you've got some explaining to do. I'd suggest you start talking fast, because as it is I'm itching to shake the truth loose from your pretty little head, which must be spinning like crazy right now."

"I—I can't talk to you when you're mad like this." She started to rise, but he pushed her back into the antique rocking chair. "You're scaring me, Sol."

"You oughta be scared, because I'm not mad." He leaned down, shoved his face an inch from hers, and whispered, "I'm furious."

Fourteen

Her teeth were chattering so hard, at first she thought it was she making the jangling sound. Suddenly realizing it was the phone, Mariah lunged for it.

Sol grabbed her wrist, knocking the receiver off the cradle.

Seizing the phone before she could, he barked into the mouthpiece "Yeah? Hello." Mariah flinched at his abrasive tone, then flinched some more when he made some barely polite small talk before shoving the receiver into her trembling hand.

"It's your sister, Beth. Says it's important. Make it fast."

Clinging to the phone as if it was a lifeline, Mariah said shakily, "What's the matter?"

"Sorry, sis." Beth's voice was hushed. "You know I wouldn't be calling if it wasn't urgent. Mom and Dad got worried and cut their trip short. They're home now, and you'd better do something quick because they took one look at your empty closet and didn't buy for a minute that you'd gone on a short trip."

The room went black and Mariah wondered if she'd fainted.

"Mariah?" Beth whispered sharply. "Mariah, are you still there?"

"Oh God," Mariah moaned. D day was at hand. "How long have they been back?"

"They've been home a few hours and grilling me the whole time. Mama's half crazed, Daddy's threatening to cut me out of his will, and I have never seen them lose their cool like this. They're positive you either ran away or lied about the annulment. If you don't get in touch by tomorrow I don't know what they'll do. Call the police maybe, or more likely the Coast Guard."

Mariah closed her eyes against the spinning room and Sol's harsh face. He was listening to her every word. First Turns and now this. It was a nightmare. No, it was worse, because this was no dream, and she was trapped in a reality that was more horrible than she'd ever feared.

"I've got to go, Mariah," Beth said. "No later than tomorrow, okay?"

"No! Don't—" *Don't leave me alone with all my lies and a husband who looks as if he'd love to skin me alive and hang me out for vulture bait.* "Talk to me some more, please, Beth."

"No can do, sis. Dad could come in my room any minute, and let me tell you, he'd probably crawl through the phone wire to drag you back home."

Mariah caught her breath. "Thanks for calling, Beth," she finally said.

"*Tomorrow.*"

"Yes."

Beth hung up but Mariah kept the receiver glued to her ear, as though it could save her from the inevitable. After a few moments Sol yanked the phone from her hands and disconnected the cord.

"So what was the emergency?" His tone was impatient, as if he were making sure no one had died before he did some killing himself.

"Nothing," Mariah said faintly. "Nothing important."

"Yeah, right. Probably no more important than my own wife treating our marriage irresponsibly and lying to me. Am I right, Mariah? Dammit, answer me! And for once, tell me the truth. If you're capable of it, you little—"

"No name-calling," she stated. Latching onto something, anything that seemed real, she began reciting his list of rules. "No in-laws, tacky—tacky presents. And you're not doing this right. Smelly socks, salt in the soup—and just a nip to begin with you said, you said nothing's insurmountable when two adults—"

"'Adults'! Listen to yourself, *baby*. The lesson's over. Now we're going to give the art of fighting some real practice. Let's just see how fast you really learn."

With a cry, Mariah surged from her chair, nearly knocking Sol down as she rushed past him.

"Hey!" he shouted. "Just where the hell do you think you're going?" He almost grabbed her, but she eluded him and ran for the door.

"I'm sorry," she sobbed out miserably. "I'm sorry, Sol. I can't stand this. I have to—to think. To get away. I'll be back, I—I promise. Please don't hate me."

The screen door slammed shut behind her and she knew only the need for escape. She couldn't see. She couldn't breathe. Nor could she hear his shouted command for her to stop as she flew blindly through the gate and into the cover of night.

Sol stared after Mariah, his bellow dying to a growl once she disappeared from view. No way he could chase after her, and he sure as hell wasn't going to air their dirty laundry in front of his folks.

He was fairly certain where she was headed, and as much as he wanted to corner her now, he'd grant her a little time to pull herself together before he set about tearing her flimsy lies apart. Besides, he didn't trust his anger. He would never hit a woman, but he was liable to say some damaging things that he wouldn't be able to take back.

Thrusting his crutches aside, Sol took several uneven steps to the rocker and reconnected the phone to make an overdue call. He was no dummy, and even a dummy could have figured out what Beth's urgent news was.

Punching out the number he hadn't dialed since he'd been overseas, Sol was rewarded with a frazzled-sounding male voice on the other end.

"Mr. Garnet . . . Oh, sorry, *Dr.* Garnet. We've never met, but I think a meeting's in order. My name's Sol Standish and your daughter just happens to be my wife. . . ."

"Oh, Hilda, Hilda, what am I going to do?" Mariah sobbed against the calf's neck in the barn lit only by a full moon. She wished she could burrow and hide and never come out, blot out the horrible memory of Sol's livid face, the sound of his fury.

"It wasn't supposed to happen like this," she moaned, clinging to Hilda. "I—I didn't mean to hurt anyone or betray Sol. It was just a little fib and then there was another one and another and—and I love him, love him so much and how can I bear it if he hates me? I can't, just can't. I can't live without him. And what if he goes to Desiree? Would he actually want to spite me so much that he'd—"

An image of Desiree soothing his wrath beat at her, causing her to shudder. "Tell me what I can I say to make everything good again, Hilda. Tell me what to do—"

"I'll tell you what to do. Get up and get in that back stall." A crutch suddenly appeared beside her bent head and Mariah jerked her tear-streaked face up to Sol. He stood over her, a giant ominously shadowed by the night. "I said get in the back stall, Mariah. And I mean *now*."

"Sol." Or was it? This wasn't the man she slept with, loved with, shared her life with. This was a dark stranger slapping her leg with a crutch when she remained paralyzed on her knees. "Please . . . please—"

"You beg pretty, little girl. But I'm not asking, I'm telling you to get your butt where I said. Don't make me move it for you."

Somehow she got up, stumbling back while he advanced, his hot breath fanning her face. She didn't know where she was going, blindly clutching stalls until she fell down on a pile of hay. The smell of fear and dread filled her senses at the sound of his crutches being thrown against wood and a gate slamming.

Then she heard the slow, deliberate rasp of leather against metal as he took off his belt.

"No, Sol!" She raised her hands as if warding off a whipping lash. "No, don't hit me, please don't—"

Leather cracked when he flung his belt away.

Before she could draw in a breath, he was between her knees, yanking up her dress and stripping off her panties. With one hand he gripped her wrists and pinned them above her head. Then his lips came down on hers and all her pleas for forgiveness were lost in his mouth.

His lips were hard and unrelenting, yet rife with a stunning passion. They rubbed against hers as his tongue stroked the softness within. Through a riot of sensation and fragmented emotion, she realized punishment was not his mission—unless punishment came in the form of a never-ending kiss, the gentle probing of his hand between her legs.

He ended the kiss, leaving her more disoriented and confused than before.

"I don't understand." She was gasping, hurting with the empty ache and the horrible lies that had brought them to this. "What do you want from me?"

"*This.*" He filled her completely with a single sleek thrust. "And more."

"More," she whimpered. Then her pinned arms were free and she was grabbing his shoulders, clutching him to her.

"That's better," he whispered harshly against her mouth. "And don't you ever suggest again that I would raise a hand to you."

"I'm sorry, Sol, sorry for everything."

"Save the apologies. The 'more' I want is some trust from my wife."

"I trust you. I—"

"Do you? Do you *really*?" He was pumping into her quick and deep, his chest pressing against her covered breasts. What was happening? He was taking her like a madman and she was wild beneath him, grateful for this plundering that took away the numbness of her body, her mind.

Defenseless, she had no choice but to cling to the trust he demanded she give and that she had been so wrong not to show long ago.

"I love you," she cried haltingly. "Trust you . . . trust—"

"Then show me. Tell me how old you are."

"Twenty . . . next year."

"Is that why you never sent Turns the birth certificate?"

"Yes. But—but I was going to, I swear it. As soon as I—I had to tell you first." His hands, as impatient as her need to tell him all, ripped the bodice of her dress. "It had to come from me."

"That it did. Though you should have told me a lot sooner." Her breasts fell into his cupped palms. His rough handling of them relayed the urgency of his need to possess and answered her need to be possessed wholly, with nothing between them.

"Hard," she demanded. "Drive it all away, Sol."

"Driving into your body is one thing, Mariah. Your mind is another, and it's vexed me, driven me half crazy the way you've given me glimpses, teasing me with what's in there, only to shut me out. Let me in now. Tell me why, *why* did you take so long to tell me the truth?"

"I was afraid you would think you'd married a kid. That you'd—decide I was too young and wouldn't want me."

"What do you take me for, a fool? One who couldn't figure out how young you were the first time we woke up in bed together with you all naked in the morning light and your makeup smeared off?" He feasted on her lips until she groaned. The sleepless nights, the self-recriminations, and all because she hadn't trusted him any more than she trusted herself.

"I was the fool, not you, Sol."

"Glad you realized that. Because the idea that I could ever give you up is about the most foolish notion I've ever heard in my life." With a snarl, he raised up and yanked off his shirt, then her dress. "So whose picture did you send me?" he asked with a grinding of his hips.

"It was . . . Beth's."

"Nice-looking woman, Beth. Ever been to Cairo, Paris—"

"No," she said. "Never. Not Pat Pong's or anyplace I said I'd been. Beth was there, not me."

"Not a family vacation, huh? And speaking of which"—he suddenly pulled out—"do your parents know we're married?"

"Don't leave me like this," she pleaded, reaching to put him back inside her. "I need you."

"You can have what you need." Sol gripped her wrist. "But not until you tell me about your parents."

"They don't know that I'm here. I told them that—" Mariah searched for and found her guts. "I told them we'd had the marriage annulled."

"Going to tell them the truth anytime soon?"

"Tomorrow. They'll try to force me to go home, Sol, but I won't go. This is my life. This is my home."

"You bet your bottom dollar this is where you belong, little lady. Because I love you. You hear me, Mariah? I love you like crazy, and nobody's taking you away from me unless it's over my dead body."

"You mean . . . you love me?" With shaking hands, she framed his face and probed his gaze. "Even after all I've done, you love me? Tell me again. *Again.*"

"I . . ." He kissed her gently. "Love . . ." He kissed her hard. "You." With one swift movement, he planted himself deep inside her, all the way to her heart. "Now that we've got that settled, I want to know the rest. You lied to me from letter one. I reckon I know why, but I want to hear it from you. Spit it out, baby."

"I didn't think you'd have anything to do with me, much less have married me."

"You're right. And for that I can forgive what you did. You made life good again for me, Mariah. I didn't want to live for a while, and now I can't live without you."

She met his thrust with a gyration of her hips, taking him in, pulling him down, getting as close to him as a desperate lover could. His rough reassurance pumped through her veins, unleashing her final confession.

"There's more, Sol. Something else you don't know about me—"

"Save it. All I want right now is a promise. No more lies. You hear me, Mariah? No more and never again. Promise me," he demanded.

"No more lies. I'll never put anything between us again. No more—" She screamed his name while her body shook. Her womb was hungry and he filled it, filled it as her final cries dissolved into a whispered sigh of "Lies."

"Mariah, wake up."

Sol's breath tickled her ear and produced an incoherent murmur from her lips. When she cuddled closer, he said, "Baby, milking time's in less than an hour, and neither of us looks exactly decent, much less proper."

"I don't care," she said groggily. "Let's roll around in the hay some more, lover."

"I must have misjudged the hour." Sol chuckled

and captured a bare breast. "Milking time just came early."

Mariah laughed throatily, gloriously sated and at peace with the world. They rolled around, limbs entangled amidst straw and discarded clothing that was ripped beyond repair.

"I love you," she vowed, sealing it with hungry kisses. "I love you, love you—"

"And I love you right back." Sol pulled away and stared down at her in the predawn light. "Can't wait to meet my new in-laws. They must be something to have raised such a unique daughter."

Mariah threw her hand over her eyes and groaned. Tomorrow had become today, and after the draining last twelve hours, dealing with her parents was the last thing she wanted to do. Not only that, but she realized her confession to Sol hadn't included an admission of her particular uniqueness.

"Sol, there's something else you deserve to know. Something about pickles and trying to save Besse and why my parents had other plans for me besides marriage."

"Yes?" he drawled. Surely that wasn't a smile tugging at his lips. "Go on, I'm all ears."

"I have a gift—well, actually it's a curse. I'm not like normal people. No matter how hard I tried to just be myself, all anyone ever cared about was my, um, peculiar abilities." She hesitated, not wanting to relinquish the normalcy she'd embraced in being simply a woman, a wife, a friend.

"I care about you, Mariah. Just for yourself."

"I know you do. You were the first one, Sol. You'll never know what freedom it meant to my life the day I went to the mailbox and opened your first letter. You didn't know anything about me but what I wanted you to know."

"A little hedging on that score, but I understand why. Now about that gift . . . ?"

"I have a photographic memory. They can't measure my IQ because it tops the scale. I have a bachelor's degree in biology and I probably could have finished medical school by now but I dragged my feet. They're still dragging. My parents are going to push hard to see that their prodigy does what they've expected all my life. But I won't go. I *won't* be a surgeon."

"Forget the parents. What I want to know is, why not? Is it because of what happened with Besse?"

Mariah shrugged, disconcerted by his demanding tone. "I failed her—"

"For the love of God, Mariah, everyone fails. It's how we learn to succeed."

"It's not just Besse. It—it's me. *Me*, Sol. For once, I can choose how to live my own life. Do you have any idea what it's like to be some—some guinea pig? To have your mind probed by experts as if it belonged to science instead of you? This is my choice. No more school, no more anything but my life with you."

She tried to push him off, to get the remains of her clothes on and leave the conversation at that. An idea had taken hold the night Besse died, but it was one to consider at her leisure, now that she was calling her own shots.

Almost. Sol pinned her with his weight and gripped her chin, which she stubbornly attempted to jerk away.

"Easy," he said firmly. "Easy, babe. We need to talk about this before you run off in a snit with your mind made up about the rest of your life. You've got some legitimate reasons to turn your back on the past, and to take some time off. But a gift like yours shouldn't be wasted."

"You sound like my parents," she accused.

"Well, this isn't them talking, it's me. I could never hold you back, any more than you could limit yourself to life on a dairy farm."

"I don't want to talk about it," she snapped. "Now let me up before someone finds us."

"Back to that, are we? A little while ago you preferred to roll around in the hay." She met his gentle teasing with a glare and a good dose of resentment for trying to take back a part of what she'd gained. "Okay," he sighed, letting her up. "But this conversation's not over. To be continued—later today, in fact."

"Absolutely not," she asserted as she dressed.

"I'm afraid you won't have any choice," Sol said from behind her. Slipping his arms around her waist, he pulled her to his chest. "Your parents are due to arrive before noon."

Fifteen

"Mariah, wait!" Sol took six steps after her, then lost his footing and had to grab the stall's swinging gate. With a growl, he limped over to his crutches while he ate Mariah's infuriated dust.

"Mornin', Dad," Sol bit out when they passed shoulders on his way from the barn.

"Where's the fire?" Herbert followed Sol's gaze across the street, where Mariah had just slammed the cottage's front door.

"I think you can see the blaze from here. Could you ask Ma to set two extra plates for dinner? We're having guests—Mariah's parents."

"I see." Herbert pulled at his chin and said slowly, "I know it's not the best time to ask, son, but should I tell your mother to prepare that fatted calf she's been saving? We've been worried you might be getting restless, since two weeks was usually your limit for R and R around here. You don't have the itch to head out soon, do you? Go see some new sights in Mobile?"

Sol considered the question; he considered the

changes in himself. "You can stop worrying, Dad. The itch got scratched and I'm here for the long haul. But you can tell Ma to save the fatted calf for breeding. There's another generation of Standishes perfectly satisfied to tend the herd."

Herbert let go of a relieved sigh. "So what're you standing around here for, boy? You've got a fire to douse before company comes to call."

"Mariah, open this door!"

"Go away," she yelled over his pounding on the bathroom door. "Just go away, you—you back-stabber."

Sinking into the claw-foot tub, she covered her ears while the water all but simmered from her boiling rage. She still couldn't believe that he'd gone behind her back, when it was her place to deal with the fiasco she'd created in Mobile. And not only that, but he'd known the truth, the whole awful truth, before putting her on the rack and grilling her.

Suddenly a click sounded and the door flew back on its hinges. Sol stood in the entry, holding the key in his hand, his expression divided between anger and heated interest in her nakedness.

"Back-stabber?" Sniffing as if he'd just picked up the scent of something foul, Sol narrowed his gaze. "No name-calling, remember?"

With a yank of the shower curtain, Mariah cut him off. A millisecond later, the curtain was jerked back and flipped over the top bar, out of her reach. Sol then proceeded to shut the toilet lid and take a seat.

"I didn't ask for an audience," she said sharply.

"And since when does a husband have to ask for one?"

"Since said husband went behind *my* back and

called *my* parents." She sat up so fast the water sloshed over the edge of the tub and onto his feet. "I can't believe you had the nerve to stick your nose where it has no business—"

"I beg your pardon? In case you forgot, we're married and that makes your business, my business. Especially when it involves some in-laws who think you ditched me."

"I had my reasons and you know it," she said. "Now look who's bending the rules, dredging up old garbage. Stick to the issue at hand, you said."

"My, my, Mariah, you *are* a fast learner. One good fight under your belt and you want to referee. But since you're turning out to be such a stickler for the rules, I'll state my case. This *is* the issue and I need to get it off my chest."

"Then get it off so you can get out."

"Well, if the kitten doesn't know how to scratch and hiss too." He leaned forward and said quietly, "Now sharpen your claws on this: You hurt me. I figured your parents might not know I existed and you snuck off once they were out of sight. But finding out they knew about me all along and you'd supposedly gotten rid of me was a damn bitter pill to swallow. Made me feel real good that you stood up for your husband like that."

"Why didn't you bring that up last night?" Her rage rapidly diminished with the sudden rush of shame and guilt.

"Because I felt you had enough to deal with and I was thinking of someone besides myself. Which is exactly what I'm asking you to do for a change."

She winced, his probing gaze making her look down.

"That's a bad habit, lady, running away from what you don't want to confront." Sol reached into the tub and flipped some water toward her face. Mariah swiped it from her cheeks and turned to him. "That's better. There's another rule, by the way. A person has to admit when he's wrong."

"Okay, I was wrong. *Wrong*," she repeated. "If I had it to do over, I'd stand up to them, but I was a different person then and our future was shaky enough without them on the scene. It was a rational decision, Sol." Shaking her head in defeat, she added, "Maybe I wouldn't do it any differently. If I had, they might have stolen any chance you were willing to give me. I'm sorry I hurt you, but can't you understand it was necessary at the time?"

She watched as he fingered his patch.

"Okay," he said begrudgingly. "I see your point. It was probably best at the time, but that time's past and I think you should grant me the courtesy of realizing I had the right to intercede by calling them last night."

"No," she said. "You had no right to do what was my responsibility."

"And if you'd taken care of it sooner I wouldn't have had any reason to assume your responsibility."

Mariah realized he *was* right, but that didn't make her like being in the wrong one bit better.

"Point to you," she admitted reluctantly. "But there's something that bothers me even more than that phone call. You knew everything before you asked me a single question last night. *You knew!* The whole time you were forcing my hand, you had the answers already, but you asked anyway. Why, Sol? Checking up to see if my conscience was in good working order or if you'd married a compulsive liar?"

"Anyone as transparent as you could use some lessons in the fine art of lying. Your conscience has been almost a living, breathing person around here. My reasons went a lot deeper than you seem to understand. Where's the soap?" Getting on his knees, he fished around the tub, between her legs and around her squirming rear before his hand emerged with the bar. He glided it down her stiffened spine.

"As we both know, Mariah, I could have come in that barn last night and laid it all out. But I wanted the truth to come from you, not them."

"Well, you got it, so I hope you're satisfied. Your methods weren't exactly nice."

"There was more at stake last night than niceties—such as what our marriage was made of if push came to shove. Lean back."

His hands were in her hair now, massaging the herbal shampoo into the hay-littered strands. How could he be so thoughtful when they were in the middle of an argument? she wondered distractedly. She wanted to hang on to her renewed anger, but the gentle fingertips tingling her scalp were making it hard.

"You scared me, backing me into the stall like that. Was that really necessary to find out what we were 'made of'?"

"I was madder than a provoked badger, baby. You'd been shutting me out long enough and I wanted the bare bones, every little wrinkle in your brilliant brain. After my chat with your father I understood enough to accept what you'd done. What I couldn't accept was anything coming between us, not when I felt I'd proven myself worthy of your trust. I got what I wanted, and don't ever try to take it back. I'll never accept anything less than all of you."

"And if I hadn't confessed, could you have accepted it?"

"No. It was a crucial moment for us, whether you realized it then or not." His thumbs were on her temples, soothing away her tension.

"What do you mean by 'crucial'? That I'd be packing my bags while you decided you had grounds for a divorce?"

Sol's face hardened. "Don't ever mention that word to me, because it never was and never will be an option for us. It's just that shading the truth to begin with was one thing, but a breach of trust at this stage would have been damaging to our marriage. We'd have had a lot more bridges to mend than what we've got to patch together now."

She knew she shouldn't say it—their emotions were too raw to dig at the sore—but say it she did.

"Enough damage for you to pay Desiree a visit—"

"Forget Desiree for once, would you? She's not the issue and is the last thing I want to think about with your parents on their way."

"Well, what about me?" Mariah shoved a finger at his chest. "Don't I count? Do you have any idea what it's like for me, knowing you were engaged to that woman?"

"How do you know that?" he demanded.

"Like you, I have my sources."

"Desiree?" he bit out. "It was Desiree, wasn't it? Dammit, I warned her—"

"Warned her?" Mariah gaped in disbelief. "Are you telling me that you've seen her or—"

"Crap!" Sol dropped his face into his hands and blew a gust of disgusted air between his lips. After long moments, he looked up. "Yes, Mariah, I have seen Desiree. And I intended to tell you as soon as—"

"All this prattling about trust and me with my dark secrets," she said through pinched lips. Her heart stumbled as jealousy, quick and acute, reared its ugly head. "So how did she look, Sol? Was she wearing anything more than her cologne when you had your rendezvous?"

"Shut up, Mariah!"

She felt as if he'd physically struck her. She blinked against the sudden sting behind her eyes and tilted up her trembling chin.

"Forget I said anything." Her voice was subdued, wounded, but carried a hint of sarcasm. "It's none of my business, of course."

"Of course it's your business." Sol caught her chin and speared her with a sharp look. "I'm sorry for lashing out at you like that, but Desiree hits a nerve with me. She's one of the blights in my life I wish didn't exist."

"But she does exist," Mariah said quietly, her hurt fading in the face of how deep his ran. "Tell me about her, Sol. Why you went to see her. Please. I need to know."

"I went to tell her to back off." Sol hesitated, then his eyes took on a distant cast. "You see, Mariah, Desiree and I go way back—even before she was head cheerleader and I was captain of the football team who lost our virginity together on homecoming night." He laughed a little cynically. "Sounds pretty trite, but that's what happened.

"Seemed the natural thing to do after what we'd been to each other. We'd played doctor as kids, and I gave her my ID bracelet in junior high. She wore my letter jacket in high school and my senior ring before I'd even worn it myself. I can still see that ugly white tape wrapped a jillion times around my ring so it wouldn't fall off her finger."

Mariah felt something thick lodge in the back of her throat. She knew too well the picture he drew, only she'd watched it from a distance. Beth had had all those things, while she'd grieved and cursed in silence because she'd craved them and had been denied.

Not that she could ever have been one of "them." But she'd deserved the right to try. Mariah swallowed against the lump of resentment. She'd resolved her envy of Beth years ago; but hearing of Desiree's past with her husband reopened the wound and filled it full of salt.

"I'm sure you made a handsome couple on homecoming night," she said, hiding her bitterness. "King and queen?"

"That's right. I scored the winning touchdown, then hit a home run in the backseat of Ma and Dad's car. I think they suspected, what with Dad tossing a box of condoms on my bed and saying, 'Whatever you do, son, just don't get that girl pregnant.' Of course, I'd had one in my billfold for over a year by then, just in case."

"And your mother?"

"She didn't approve of Desiree any more than Dad, not that Ma was impolite to her. She just had a way of waiting up for me on my dates and saying for as long as I can remember, 'She's not for you, son. Wait for the right girl.' Not that my hormones listened. And being a teenager I felt a sense of independence by going against their wishes."

"You mean, the less they approved, the more you did."

"Exactly." The look he gave Mariah conveyed his belief that she was presently guilty of the same rebellion against her own parents—and him. "Anyway, I won a football scholarship to the University of Wisconsin in Madison, and that put several hundred miles between us."

"Desiree didn't follow you?"

"She did, but she decided to major in clothes, parties, and sex—with other guys. She flunked out the first year, and not even her daddy's money could get her back in."

"Too bad," Mariah muttered sarcastically.

"Best thing that ever happened to me, though it hurt like hell when I found out she was fooling around. And I can't tell you how relieved my folks were. Predictably, Desiree and I grew apart."

"You mean you grew and she stagnated, waiting for you."

"Desiree doesn't give up that easy. For a long time, even after I broke up with her, she burned up the phone wires trying to keep tabs on me, and she had a way of driving down in her new sports car unannounced on weekends. Found me in bed once with a girl. Whew, what a scene. Anyway, after I graduated I came home and saw her for what she really was. She hadn't changed a bit and I realized she never would. I lost all my respect for her then. She'd developed quite a reputation as an easy lay around here. You pretty much know what happened right after that."

"You signed up and took off."

"Yep."

When he didn't continue, Mariah's brow furrowed. "There's more, isn't there? I mean, you were engaged."

"Unfortunately, yes. Two years ago, my father's nightmare came true. I got Desiree pregnant."

Mariah stared at him. Her stomach bottomed out.

"Did you lose your wallet?" she asked, unable to stop the jealous, petty remark. Sol winced, then frowned.

"I didn't know you then. And believe me, I more than paid for my stupidity. I was here on leave, and

I got into an old argument with Dad about why I didn't want to stay and work on the farm. I walked out on him, went to a bar, and got plastered. Desiree was there and she . . . made herself available to me. A month later when I was back overseas, I got a phone call from her that wiped me out. I didn't hesitate to ask her to marry me. The fact that I didn't love her made no difference. Owning up to my responsibilities did."

"I wouldn't expect any less of you, Sol." Even as she said it, Mariah cringed at the thought of how dangerously close she'd come to losing him. "What happened? Did she miscarry?"

"She aborted it," he said in a flat tone. Mariah made a strangled sound. "Oh, she insisted it was a miscarriage when I confronted her with it, but she'd already confided in her best friend, who just couldn't keep such a juicy piece of gossip to herself. News travels fast in a small town, and my parents made sure it reached me."

"How horrible. Why did she do it? Why—"

"Desiree's very figure-conscious, so maybe she was worried she wouldn't fit into her wedding gown. Hell, who knows with her? And she never did like kids. Anyway, I was coming home in a few weeks for the wedding, and I'm sure she didn't plan on telling me about the baby until after we'd gotten married. Fortunately, I found out sooner."

"Thank God," Mariah whispered, then laid a comforting hand on his knee. "I'm sorry, Sol."

Sol nodded sadly and sighed heavily. "Well, that's the story. It's done and over with and a part of my life I'm glad to have behind me. If you've got any more questions about Desiree, spit them out now. I don't want to go through all this again because it gives me an ill feeling to remember it."

"No," Mariah said slowly, "no more questions about Desiree, Sol. And I promise not to bring her up again, since I know the truth."

"Then we'll call ourselves even. *Now*," he said decisively, "enough about my dark secrets. We've got two frantic parents who are going to be here in a few hours and will doubtless do their best to wedge us apart. That's why they're coming, you know—to try to make you see reason and take you back to *their* home."

"Well, it's not mine. Not anymore and never again."

"That's right, so just keep that in mind while they're here. Our unsettled business can wait; theirs can't. For the time being we put our problems on hold, slap a smile on our faces, and pretend everything's hunky-dory."

"You're right—we do need to present a united front." Curious, she added, "What did you tell them, anyway?"

"Not much. Just that I'd convinced you to remarry me while they were gone and we were eager to have them visit our home so they could see how happy we are."

"You covered for me," she said in disbelief. "Why?"

"You're my wife, that's why. And while I was at it, Beth got a break too. Your father said she'd concocted another story, so I explained that it was our doing for wanting to give them the big news ourselves. As for the other interesting topics— particularly your 'gift'—I insinuated I already knew and that we'd discuss everything once they arrived."

"I don't believe it. You took up for me when you had every reason not to."

"For such a genius, love, you've been a little slow

on the uptake. It's what I've been trying to tell you—we stick together no matter what." He got up with unexpected ease, and reached for a towel. "Lying goes against my grain," he continued, "just as nodding your head and going along with anything I say or do today likely will with you. Do it anyway. Understood?"

Her hair rinsed, Mariah got out of the tub. Sol patted her dry, lingering over her breasts and the V of her thighs. He started to wrap the towel about her, then discarded it to take in her nakedness.

"I understand." She understood plenty. He wanted to kiss and make up. They weren't through with certain issues, not by a long shot, but given his unstinting support, when a lesser man would have dumped her in the mess she'd made instead of cleaning up after her, Mariah decided she'd gladly give him a kiss. Kisses were good for hurts, too, and she wanted to ease away the pain she and Desiree had caused him.

Stretching out in feline fashion, she felt a glowing tingle spread over her skin. The girl who had run on their honeymoon night was now a woman who stood here without modesty, wearing nothing but an expression of pleasure in his appreciative gaze, which now darkened with purpose.

She needed to bond with him in that purpose, to join intimate forces before confronting the opposition. She and Sol were strong. His strength came from years and experience; hers may have been there all along, but only under his guidance was she swiftly coming into her own.

Laying her hand over his arm, she gripped him tight. "Together we stand," she vowed.

"And divided we fall. Whatever you do, don't dispute me in front of your parents. Wait until we're alone." His smile was brief; his caress of her breast anything but. "These first-year dues are hell to pay, aren't they?"

"They are." Hastily unbuttoning his shirt, she pressed a kiss to his scar. "But no pain, no gain. And strange as it is, I feel that we've gotten a dividend from our mistakes. That somehow we're more than what we were." Resting her head against his chest, she felt his arms come around her and his lips nuzzle her hair.

"Here I thought I knew so much about settling differences, and you go expanding the rules. Marriage being a lifelong deal, we should be real smart by the time we advance to even bigger and better mistakes."

She dreaded them already. Then again, perhaps it was true that the bumps and jolts along the way were more important than a too-easy ride. *I needed to find out what our marriage was made of if push came to shove.* His words came back to her with new meaning.

"You went against your principles for me, even though I've done little to deserve it," she said. "I'm sorry for more than my deceit—my lack of faith in you as a person and a mate deserves an apology too. What we are is not weak, Sol. I owe you for making me realize that, among other things."

"You owe me nothing, because you're my wife."

"Even without the marriage certificate?"

"What kind of crazy talk is that, woman? Of course you're my wife. That's just a piece of legalese confirming the vows we already took." He stamped his assertion with a kiss, then moved away. "We've got a few hours before they get here. Let's go build on the ammunition we've already got."

Mariah blinked. She must be seeing things. *Impossible.* He *couldn't* have taken those two steps before retrieving his crutches and hooking a thumb in the bedroom's direction. Could he?

Sixteen

"Care for a beer, Tom? Wine, Nita?"

"None for me, thank you," Dr. Garnet said. "Nita?"

Nita Garnet shook her head, her gaze remaining on Mariah and Sol. "Iced tea might be nice."

"Baby, you care to brew some for your mother?"

Mariah forced herself to smile. The introductions, made while her parents had openly stared at Sol's crutches and patch, had been strained enough; Sol calling them by their first names instead of addressing them as "Doctor and Mrs." heightened the underlying tension. And now she was biting her tongue to keep from saying she wasn't about to leave the room. Sol had a propensity for bluntness, and Mariah knew diplomacy was the best way to handle her parents.

When she hesitated, Sol prompted, "Mariah, the tea?"

"Oh, of course, darling," she said. As she moved past him, Sol caught her hand and pulled her down for a kiss. Mariah stiffened when he lengthened it and patted her rear end affectionately *in front of her parents!* By the time she exited to the kitchen, her anxiety had increased tenfold.

Between putting on the kettle and fiddling with tea bags, Mariah kept her ears glued to the door.

"Nice farm," her father said brusquely.

"We like it. Three generations strong and more on the horizon, Tom. You and Nita will have to visit often. Especially once grandchildren enter the big picture."

"'Grandchildren'?" her mother echoed with dismay. Peeking around the corner, Mariah saw her mother sweeping back her lovely hair, her equally perfect beauty scored by a "surely you can't be serious" expression. "Years in the future, perhaps, but Mariah's still a child. She has no business bearing children until she's embraced her destiny."

"Her destiny is her own, Nita," Sol said flatly. Mariah fought the urge to bound into the living room to cheer; at the same time she wanted to gag him and diffuse the escalating turbulence with some tact.

"Beyond that," he continued, "we decide when and where our future lies, and that includes offspring. No disrespect intended, but did either of you ask your parents' permission to get married, to get pregnant, where you could live, or what profession to pursue?"

Mariah clamped a hand over her mouth. Good Lord, he'd actually said *that* to *them!* Innuendo was one thing, but such deliberate head-bashing was beyond her parents' standard of acceptable behavior.

"Now see here, young man," Tom Garnet said. "This is our daughter you're talking about, and she's certainly no ordinary young girl, not to mention—"

"Not to mention, I'm her husband. And while we're on the subject of being ordinary, if you'd given her a chance at living an *ordinary* life, she might not have sought refuge with me. Back off, Tom. Chill out, Nita. Mariah needs some room to breathe and she's a grown woman, perfectly able to make her own decisions. In fact, I say we get her in here now to do just that."

Rushing back to the boiling water, Mariah filled two cups and wished she could jump in there with them. Oh, this was worse than she'd imagined, and Sol, for all his good intentions, was doing a doozy of a job at alienating her family. She wouldn't have gone about it his way, not at all.

"Mariah! Baby, get your bu—self back here."

"Yes?" Mariah emerged with a smile stretched from one ear to the other. "What is it, Sol, uh, dear?"

"Are you of sound mind?" His gaze was leveled at Tom.

"Of course. My mind is in perfectly good working order."

"Are you unhappy with me, our life on this farm?"

"I couldn't be happier," she said with conviction. Reaching for Sol's hand, she clung to the strength they had won and that she desperately needed now.

"But would you be happier in medical school? Say, go back with these fine parents of yours, see me on holidays, then return here in a couple of years, since it shouldn't take you any longer than that to get your degree and hang your shingle."

Mariah looked from her father's glowering face to her mother's pale one to Sol's calm expression.

"Mariah," said her father firmly, "you surely can't turn away from what you were born for to settle for this man's limited vision and—"

"And, sweetheart, your daddy and myself, we both want you to be happy, but you must realize that you're still so young to be making these decisions.

Go pack your things and we'll discuss this in Mobile tomorrow."

"Your mother's right," Tom said. "Nineteen is no age to turn your back on the world when the medical community can gain so much from your gift. That's selfish and immature, young lady. We raised you for more than this—*this* man who's older than your Uncle David and has the manners of a white-trash punk."

Mariah gaped at her father. Indignation rose so swiftly in her, she was momentarily speechless. To think she had been upset with Sol for his tactics, when it was her father who stooped to tasteless slurs.

"How *dare* you," she gritted out, her eyes snapping fire. "How dare you speak of *my* husband in those terms. Never, and I mean *never* say anything like that again. If you do, you can forget this daughter exists."

Sol took her hand and squeezed it. The gesture, she realized, was more than support. It was also silent applause. And then something else came to her. Sol had deliberately put her in the position of having to choose sides.

She chose.

"My mind is my own, and so is my life, whether you like it or not," she went on. "How I choose to live it might be of interest to you, but it's no longer your business. I love you, Mother and Daddy, but I love my husband as an adult, not a child. As a woman I'm responsible for *my* decisions, and my decision is to stay here, with Sol. I stand by his words—we decide our own future. Now you decide whether or not to be part of it."

"Of course we want to be, but your training, your exceptional talent—"

"Mariah, you can't just throw it all away—"

"Why don't you both just back off—"

"Stop it!" she shouted over their raised voices. "All of you. I've had it, don't you understand? *This* is my husband. This is *my* life. Sol and I are married and that's final." She stared them down, then said calmly, "Now, if you'll excuse me, the tea's brewed and LaVerne—Mom—is expecting us for dinner soon."

"Mom?" Nita said with a measure of hurt. "*I* am your mother, not some stranger you've recently met, Mariah Garnet."

"*Standish*, Mother. Mariah Standish, if you please, or even if you don't please. And I would thank you to remember that *Mom* has been more hospitable to me than any Southern hospitality committee ever thought about being. If you've got a problem with that, then I think it's time you drove back to the airport and we all get on with our separate lives."

Nita turned as if in slow motion to Tom, who appeared to be past coherent speech. Their state of shock was immensely gratifying to Mariah, at the same time as she was shocked at herself. And sorry that she hadn't set her foot down sooner. She just wished she hadn't had to hurt them in the process. They meant well, but were too accustomed to getting their way in what they perceived as her best interests.

"The tea, love?" Sol pulled her onto his lap in an overtly possessive and most improper display that was surprisingly more liberating than embarrassing. Then, to her ear he whispered, "Bravo, baby. You skedaddle and I'll take it from here."

"Mariah," her father called as she veered triumphantly toward the kitchen, "I'll take that beer if it's still available."

"And while you're at it, dear," her mother added faintly, "could you forget the tea and make mine wine? Or better yet, a gimlet—maybe a double?"

"Bye, Mother and Daddy. Come see us soon!"

"The welcome mat's always out, Tom and Nita," Sol intoned. "Don't be strangers. And don't forget to send me Mariah's birth certificate."

The car backed up and Sol pulled Mariah closer while her parents waved a last farewell. She was still amazed by all the man-to-man handshaking and her mother's teary hugs and kisses. In all her years of living under the same roof with her parents, she'd never witnessed such gushing displays of affection.

"Whew," Sol muttered as soon as the car was out of sight. "That was one helluva coup we pulled off, kiddo. But you know them better than I do—think they left satisfied?"

"More satisfied than I dreamed possible," she said with a relieved sigh. "I never would have taken them on the way you did. They weren't the only ones with their jaws on the floor when you brought out the big guns and plunked me in the middle of the line of fire."

"Made you squirm, huh?" He squeezed her behind until she squirmed some more and batted at his hand.

"Squirm and want to crawl into a bottomless pit until they were gone and you quit behaving like a punk." With a sidelong glance at Sol, she broke into an ear-splitting grin.

"A punk on purpose. And you *didn't* crawl away. I'm always proud of you, Mariah, but I was never prouder than when you threw your lot in with me and stuck up for yourself. I didn't like putting you in that position, but I thought it best."

"Your way *was* best. If I had been handling it, we'd still be hedging around the real issues with nothing hashed out and our brains splitting from headaches." Then, suddenly remembering some of Sol's more dubious negotiating tactics, she spun around and confronted him, her grin fading.

"But just what did you mean by telling them *you* would see to my continued education? And to send my birth certificate to *you?* I'm not going back to school, and I made a copy of my own birth certificate before I even came here."

"Good, then we can put it into the mail first thing tomorrow," Sol said around a yawn. "Let's hit the hay, woman, minus the straw. I'm beat."

"Just a minute, Sol. You didn't answer my question about why you told them you'd see that I went back to school. I kept my mouth shut because I promised to go along with anything you said and settle whatever I took exception to later. I take exception to that, and 'later' is now."

"Mariah, it's been a long, draining day, and last night was no walk in the park. This can wait until we're ready to deal with it. I feel like I've been put through the spin cycle on a heavy-duty washer, and surely you do too. Let's go to bed. I could use a few hugs and some more make-up kisses."

"No, it *can't* wait, and you can forget any hugs and kisses until you tell me you were placating them with that line of tripe. I got the feeling that parting handshake with my father had something to do with a meeting of minds I wasn't privy to."

"It's not tripe, Mariah." Sighing heavily, Sol grasped her shoulders and said firmly, "You *are* going to med school. I asked your father to see that your transcripts were forwarded to the school nearest us, which is only about an hour's drive. He assured me that with his pull and your credentials he could get you in, no problem. I didn't realize the leading institutions had been fighting for the exclusive rights to you. Though I don't know why I should be surprised—you haven't quit amazing me since the day we met."

"I don't believe you!" Fighting the impulse to lunge at him, she poked his chest with a finger. "How *dare* you make decisions that are mine, and mine alone, to make. Not only that, you did it knowing full well I've had enough education to last me a lifetime. I told you that and yet you go acting as authoritarian as my parents. I didn't leave them just to hook up with an overbearing substitute."

Sol looked down at her finger. "Why do I get the impression that since you've had a taste of independence, you're feeling your oats? I liked you better when you were facing down Tom and Nita."

"And I don't like you at all right now," she shot back.

"Suit yourself, *kid.* But this 'overbearing substitute' has reason to think you're rebelling to assert what you perceive as maturity. Here's a news flash from someone who's already tread that hot wire and come back. Being mature means acting as a responsible adult."

"I *am* a responsible adult, and I expect you to treat me like one."

"I will, as soon as you realize that means seeing beyond your own needs. It extends to those depending on you, and the challenge of returning what gifts we're given to the world-at-large. Your parents admitted to being wrong about a lot of things, but they were right about that."

Resisting the urge to cover her ears, to spit on the ground and throw her cursed gift in God's face, Mariah asserted her freedom to choose.

"I don't want the gift. Let someone else have it and go in my place to med school. Someone who wants to be there, because I won't. What I've got now is plenty to suit me."

Sol shook his head with a maddeningly patient know-all, see-all certainty. "You can't give your talents away, and even if you could, *I* can't ignore what's there. You're a remarkable woman, Mariah, and I'm damn lucky to have you for my wife. But waste is a sin, one I can't stomach. And, if you're as adult as you say you are, neither can you."

"I didn't ask for your philosophy on life, mortal sin, or what you can or can't stomach, fella. They can all take a hike as far as I'm concerned, because no one but me is running my life—not even you."

"Grow up," he snapped. "Because as long as you're bent on hanging on to such selfish illusions, I'll be as bullying and authoritarian as I have to be until you own up to what's right. In other words, you *are* going back to school—even if I have to drag you every step of the way."

Seventeen

"The pickles are ready for sampling, honey, and I think you deserve the first bite."

"Thanks, Mom," Mariah said dully, then tasted their efforts from nearly a month before . . .

Before she'd bared her soul in the barn. Before the medical school had contacted her about a "sudden" opening. Before her parents had begun calling every few days and sending loads of wedding presents, along with good wishes to their beloved daughter and "such an impressive, mature, and charming—please forgive us for our unforgivable slurs—husband," whom they wholly approved of, now that she didn't.

Time had marched on, and if practice made perfect, she and Sol were now pros in the fine art of arguing.

"What's wrong, honey? Missing your folks? After I married Herbert, I was homesick a good two years before I resigned myself to the fact that I was grown up and Herbert wasn't putting up with any more of my goings-on, whining, as he put it."

"Sounds like Sol takes more after him than you, Mom."

"That he does. Herbert and I wanted more babies, but it wasn't meant to be. Of course, Sol was about three rolled into one."

"He likes to 'roll,' all right. Now that 'over hill and dale' are behind him, he's advanced to steamrolling over me."

"Figured as much. Another pickle, Mariah?" Mariah waved away the offering. "What's eating at you, girl? The pickle's just fine, so I take it the same doesn't apply to you and my son."

Feeling as if she would burst from the pressure if she didn't unload, Mariah took LaVerne into her confidence.

"Mom, it's a mess. Since my parents took off, Sol and I can't agree on anything but arguing and then putting our differences aside long enough to—" Mariah cleared her throat awkwardly. "Long enough to kiss and make up before we get into it all over again."

"I'm a woman, same as you, Mariah, and in that we've got common ground. My son aside, men are what they are and women . . . well, what's the harm in letting them think they've got the upper hand, so long as they play into yours?"

Mariah studied her mother-in-law. She was a bit stunned that something so calculating could have come from LaVerne's salt-of-the-earth soul.

"Don't you think that's a rather manipulative way to deal with other people?"

"We're not talking about 'other people,' honey. We're talking about husbands, men who like to call the shots. Sol's like his daddy—unbending once he gets his mind set on something. Won't listen to reason or budge an inch. That's why, to bring them around and still keep the peace, we have to handle them a certain way."

Spearing another pickle, Mariah leaned closer to LaVerne. "Let me get this straight. What you're telling me is that there's a technique to working out your differences with an overbearing man that my husband failed to mention?"

"Overbearing? Why, Mariah, surely you realize they perceive themselves as fair and just." Chuckling, LaVerne wagged her finger. "And, of course, they are—at heart. They're just a little nearsighted when it comes to compromise sometimes. That's why we have to pull a few tricks to make them see the light. It's for their own good. And, of course, for ours too."

Sifting through this interesting strategy, Mariah drummed her fingers on the table. "Okay, Mom. You've got my attention."

"And attention is exactly what you've got to get. Any man who's in love with a woman—and it's plain to see that Sol's head over heels in love with you—has a weak spot, and you have to hit it just right."

"Well, it can't be the head, because his is too hard to crack."

"That's right, so you use what he can't compete against." LaVerne winked. "There's a dance in town next week. Now, I'd suggest to you that we girls approach our husbands about needing a night out. How are you fixed for a party dress?"

"I've got several sundresses, church dresses, and a drawerful of jeans that I wear all the time. . . ." Realizing Sol rarely saw her in anything else, and that she'd even forsaken makeup in her acclimation to the country life, Mariah was disturbed that she'd neglected her feminine side. "Actually, Mom, I could use a new dress."

"Now you're cooking with gas." LaVerne motioned her toward the sewing room. "I've got a pattern in here that's just out of this world and should guarantee you Sol's undivided attention. Once you've got that, see if he doesn't soften up enough to listen."

"New dress, babe?"

"Like it?" Mariah said in a husky, sensual voice. As she slowly pivoted in front of the porch swing he'd been impatiently lounging on while she finished getting ready, Sol took inventory of his wife.

At least he assumed it was Mariah, with her hair a wild mass of fluffed-out curls, makeup that transformed her sweet features into those of a knockout. And a dress that revealed too much cleavage, too much leg, and hugged her behind too tightly for a public place.

"It's, uh . . . something else," he said hoarsely, wondering if every other man's tongue at the dance was going to be trailing the ground too. Hell, he could taste the dirt already.

"Sure you don't want to drive with Ma and Dad?" At least in the backseat he could get his hands on some of that leg and those creamy shoulders, which were bare except for two straps that looked as though they might snap any minute from the strain of her bosom.

"I'd rather drive alone with you," she said in an unusually provocative tone, then proceeded to walk toward him with an equally provocative sway of her hips. He'd heard about Miss Lilah and her finishing school, but he was certain Mariah's strut was not part of the graduating criteria.

Placing two sets of ruby-painted nails on his shoulders, she leaned over him, and he got a clear shot of that bosom. Sol made a muffled sound of distress, having been reduced from speech to barely contained grunts.

Tracing his lips with her tongue, she darted it inside his mouth and took it back before he could claim it. With a quick nip of his bottom lip, she straightened and smiled sexily while her mascara-laced lashes coyly drooped. Good Lord! Where had his child bride gone to? There was not a hint of her in this femme fatale who not only made his pants feel too tight, but also expanded his conception of just who his wife was.

"If we drive alone," she said, sounding smooth and sweet as honey, "we can have more privacy, and I would like that. Wouldn't you, darling?"

"Umm . . . sure." At the moment, if she'd said that cows could fly, he would have agreed in a heartbeat. When she angled her gaze at his crotch before reaching for his crutches, Sol said raggedly, "Privacy's definitely a good idea. Sure you want to go to this dance, babe?"

"Oh, yes. We've never really had a date, so this will be like our first. I wouldn't miss it for the world."

That she was right struck him then. They'd never had a real courtship. Being married to her from the start, he hadn't considered her need to be romanced and sweet-talked.

"You know, Mariah, sometimes I amaze myself with my own insensitivity. Let's get out of here, gorgeous. It's past time I showed you the time of your life."

"You *are* my life, Sol," she murmured. "At least, I never felt truly alive until you came into it."

Her simple statement bounced in his head, and he stared at her as if for the first time. Seeing her with her lips tilted in a serene Mona Lisa smile, he realized that this was not the same woman he'd married. This Mariah was no girl, but a self-possessed woman who was lush and in full bloom. She'd come into her own, and she wore her many colors well.

When had it happened? Had the transformation been slow, or an overnight exchange of a cocoon for wings? Wings that, unlike his, had never had the opportunity to truly fly—even away from him!

All this hit him with a jolt that came closer to a sickening thud. Obsessed by his gnawing concerns, Sol was hardly aware of the miles sliding beneath the truck.

Mariah rolled down her window and nuzzled close to his side. "Ah, smell this air," she said. "I feel high. High and free enough to spread my arms and coast on the wind."

Sol kept a possessive arm wrapped around her shoulders. When they pulled into the dance hall parking lot, he tightened his grip.

Music spilled from the open doors.

It taunted his ears and played havoc with his new awareness. The song summed up his inner distress: "They Call the Wind Maria."

Eighteen

"Long time no see, Sol. Heard you got married, but no one said you had such a foxy wife. She's beautiful."

"How're you doing, Hank? Meet Mariah." Sol reached for his beer and guzzled the brew while Mariah glanced uncertainly from his brooding scowl to Hank.

"How do you do, Hank?" she said as graciously as she'd greeted the other men she'd been introduced to. "Would you care to join us?" It seemed the polite thing to say, she thought, and maybe Sol would change his strange behavior if they had company. At least *she'd* have someone to talk to. Since they'd walked in, he'd hardly said anything, besides telling her to pull down her skirt and push up her top. She'd just as soon forget him snapping that she ought to go wash her face.

"Thanks," Hank said, "but my favorite polka just started. Sol, you mind if I ask your lady to dance?"

"Go ahead," he said curtly. "She's been tapping her foot since we got here, and she hasn't hit the dance floor yet. Not that she hasn't had every Tom, Dick, and hairy stud in town asking her to boogie."

Hank took a step back, his friendly smile wavering.

"Thanks anyway, Hank, but I'll sit this one out," Mariah told him. "Maybe another time." As soon as he was gone, Mariah gripped Sol's wrist as he reached for the nearly empty pitcher. "What *is* the matter with you?" she hissed.

"What's the matter with me?" he hissed back. "I'll tell you what *is* the matter with me. My wife's got every damn male hormone in the joint dancing a jig in his pants instead of on the dance floor, when she's supposedly with me."

"I *am* with you, though Hilda would be better company than you've been the last hour."

"Maybe all that lash-batting and 'Oh, so delighted to meet you, won't you please join us' flirting you've been so generous with has a bit to do with it."

"Flirting? Flirting! I've been polite and gracious, that's all. Mostly to make up for your lack thereof. You've embarrassed me, Sol, acting so abrupt and sulking in your beer. I'd hoped we could have a good time."

"Yeah? Well, while we're on the topic of alcohol consumption, what about the fact that you're underage but you've got so much makeup on you haven't been carded? And you've been slamming down that wine like a Frenchie on a binge."

Mariah could barely contain her anger. "I wouldn't exactly call two glasses in nearly as many hours 'slamming it down.' And since when was the way I wear my makeup a concern of yours?"

"Since you started dressing like a vamp who's advertising her wares and giving it away for free."

"What? Your mother made this dress for me and I wore it to look nice for you—"

"Nice? You call that *nice?* I like your jeans ten times better and your face scrubbed clean."

Mariah's jaw worked back and forth as if she were chewing nails. She was furious and absolutely dumbfounded by Sol's ridiculous behavior. This wasn't working out at all the way it was supposed to. She was hurt and so disappointed she wanted to cry, hit something, especially *him*, for destroying what was meant to be special and to mend their bridges, which were crumbling before her disbelieving eyes.

"I know what your problem is." Mariah was suffering, and she wanted him to feel the pain he'd caused. "You're jealous. You're jealous because everyone's asking me to dance and you can't. The truth is, if you wanted to, you could. You're just too proud to do it with your crutches and let me lead. Now, we can either leave or start the night from scratch. Take your pick because—"

"Miss?" A cocktail waitress extended a glass of wine. "This was sent from that gentleman at the bar, miss."

"*Mrs.*" Sol's lips barely moved.

Mariah looked from the glass to Sol's sullen expression, then to the handsome stranger waving from the bar. Sol said nothing more. Mariah debated her answer while the barmaid set a cocktail napkin on the table.

Sol had promised her the night of her life, and it was a night she needed. For once in her life, *she* wanted to feel like the homecoming queen with her king. He'd given Desiree that; didn't she deserve as much? Or at least more than him glaring at her while other couples hugged at tables, clung to each other on the dance floor, toasted with frothy mugs in the muted glow of candlelight.

"Thank you," Mariah said to the waitress. "And please, thank the sender."

She took a sip, fully aware of the challenge in her small action. Other men wanted to treat her nicely; maybe it would rub off on her husband.

Mariah studied him over the rim of her glass. *Surely* Sol had enough sense to realize that women responded best to a show of respect, manners, and courtesy. If Sol was too dense for her words to sink in, surely this action should tell him to set aside his peeves and to act as maturely as he'd insisted she should.

When his glare intensified to a seething stare, Mariah decided that making her point wasn't worth it. As much as she hated it, she'd stoop to placating him to salvage the night.

"Come on, Sol," she said. Putting down her glass, Mariah gestured to the dance floor. "Dance with me. Please?"

Sol lowered his mug between them with a *thud.*

"Enjoy your drink, Miss Manners. I need to go to the can, then get a little fresh air. The stuff I'm breathing in here isn't as fresh and pure as I'm used to." Grabbing his crutches, he was out of his chair before she could blink. "Your not-so-secret admirer's on his way over, no doubt to ask you to dance. Don't let me cramp your style."

Mariah stared after Sol's retreating back, her mouth agape. What was the matter with him? And what was the matter with her, letting him treat her so horribly? She deserved better than this. She deserved all the dances Desiree had enjoyed with him and she'd never had. Even *one* would—

"Care to dance?"

Mariah looked up into the stranger's face, then at the hand he extended. He was a little flushed, maybe from the heat, maybe from the alcohol.

Either way, she didn't care. Not when Sol expected her to kowtow to his ego even though her own was in a shambles. Maybe a little competition wouldn't hurt, would shake him out of his stupid and juvenile pettiness. Maybe he'd even be jealous enough to break in.

"Would I like to dance?" she repeated with a forced smile. "No, I'd *love* to dance."

Mariah took her partner's hand and flew with bitter wings that flapped upon a dying wind.

Sol took a breath of fresh air and checked his watch. He'd been gone twenty minutes—long enough to get a grip on the frustration and the fear gnawing at his gut.

And long enough for Mariah to have a few dances with some men, the kind of experience she should have had before hooking up with him. She'd never even been to a prom, she'd confided on the drive over. Never had more than a few dates with some other "eggheads," she'd said. He'd known she was inexperienced, but not to that extent.

His heartbeat swished dully between his ears as he opened the door to the dance hall. He was testing her, he supposed, pushing and bullying, acting like a total jerk. A jerk who was afraid of losing her, now that she'd grown into her new skin, afraid she would realize there were better bargains than him out there. He'd deliberately given her the chance to spread her wings without him around. Noble?

No. Selfish. He'd wanted to assure himself she'd still be waiting for him, that even at his worst she wouldn't want anyone but him. If she was still at the table he would apologize. Hell, he'd even ask her to dance and make an ass of himself with his crutches on the dance floor. If he were just a little more confident of his strength, he'd ditch them and sweep her off her feet, the way he'd been dreaming of doing all night.

When their table came into sight, Sol's heart plummeted. His mother was sitting where Mariah had been.

"Where is she?" Sol demanded.

"And just where the hell have you been, young man?"

"Outside. Now where is she?"

"Sit down," LaVerne snapped. "There's something I want you to watch until you can learn some manners and the proper way a man should treat his wife."

Sol sat, knowing he wouldn't get any answers out of his mother until he did. "Did Dad take her home?"

"Why should he when she's having a good time? No thanks to you. That poor girl was practically in tears by the time you left. Shame on you."

"I'm ashamed enough of myself, Ma. Now where is she?"

He stopped searching the crowd long enough to glance at his mother, and saw a hint of pleasure in her face.

"She's dancing, son. Tore up the floor with a polka and three different partners. I believe the one she started out with just broke in again for a waltz." Sol shoved his seat back, but LaVerne gripped his arm. "Oh, no you don't. You're going to sit here and watch just a bit. You've poured enough castor oil down her throat; now let her enjoy herself before you decide to ruin the fun she'd expected from you."

LaVerne pointed her finger at the crowd, and Sol zeroed in on a glimpse of Mariah's face, her cheeks rosy from exertion, her lips tilted coyly as she smiled at her partner. When he suddenly dipped her, she laughed with delight.

Sol's heart dipped along with her body. In reflex, he reached for his crutches, but LaVerne intercepted.

"Stay put, son. The next dance just got started."

The minutes ticked by leadenly while Sol strained to keep his gaze locked on Mariah as she swayed through the crowd. With each glimpse of her passing from one partner to another, his insides squeezed until they felt like pulp.

Mariah was the wind. Mariah was spreading her wings.

Mariah was his wife. His wife, dammit. She didn't want to go to med school? Fine. She wanted to dress herself up like a model and work a crowd? Fine. He'd give her whatever freedom she wanted.

Any freedom at all, except freedom from him.

"I've seen enough," Sol gritted out. This time when he reached for his crutches, LaVerne only shrugged.

"If you plan to break in, you'd better hurry. It's a slow dance, so maybe you'll get there in time to finish it and treat her as nice as the partner she's got now."

Sol was already elbowing his way forward. Ignoring the shouts of "Hey, watch where you're going!" and "Where you been, Sol? Buy you a beer?" and "Ain't that your wife kicking up her heels? I get the next dance after you!" thrown his way, Sol pushed and shoved without so much as an "Excuse me."

All he could see was the top of Mariah's head; she'd rested her face on another man's shoulder. Sol felt himself filling up with so much possessiveness and self-reproach he couldn't think beyond getting to her and tearing her away from the lech's hands that were straying down her back to the rise of her buttocks.

In a minute that seemed like an hour, Sol broke through the dancing couples and clamped a hand on a broad shoulder.

"Hey, go break in on someone else," his rival growled, without bothering to turn around. When he tried to shake off Sol's iron-tight grip, Sol practically knocked him to the floor. The action sent Mariah stumbling against a nearby couple while her partner jumped to his feet, whirled around, and raised a fist.

With lightning-quick reflexes, Sol caught and twisted it. His gaze was a menacing, lethal, pinpoint glare.

"Unless you want a broken arm, you'd better clear this floor and never even *think* about laying a hand on *my* wife again. That behind you were feeling up belongs to me."

"Your wife?" The loudly spoken words rose over the music. Several heads turned as murmurs rippled through the crowd. Dancers backed up and started clearing the floor. The singer's voice trailed off, followed by the guitar, then the drum. The piano ended in mid-chord.

Silence. Except for the rasp of Mariah's uneven breathing and the drunken chuckle of Sol's opponent, whom Sol was glad he didn't know.

"You heard me," Sol said between clenched teeth. "My wife." He wanted nothing more than to break the jerk's arm in two, but the guy was drunk, and it wouldn't be a fair fight. Deciding he'd made his point, Sol let go. "Go find another partner. The one you had is taken—she's mine."

The other man looked around and grew red in the

face, obviously humiliated and unwilling to give Sol the last word.

"Then take her," he announced to the crowd more than Sol. Gesturing to the crutches, he challenged, "Why don't you dance with her yourself? Oughta take better care of your woman, if you ask me." Then, jabbing a finger in the direction of Sol's patch, he bellowed, "Or can't you see for yourself you've got a good thing in this little missy?"

Sol looked past him to Mariah's stricken face. "I see exactly what I've got. And as for suggesting that dance, I've never heard such a smart idea come out of any drunk's mouth."

He thrust his crutches at the drunk, who caught them as he weaved his way off the floor. Sol heard him slur, "Hey, man, you're gonna need these to dance with your lady."

"Keep 'em. I've got a wedding dance that's long past due." With his eye locked on Mariah, he took a single step forward, and then another. Her expression of disbelief, of wonder at seeing a miracle, kept him going. Her moist eyes blinked, then blinked again, as if she couldn't trust what she was seeing. With tears on her lashes, she held out her arms. Whether she was asking him in or wanting to catch him should he fall, he wasn't sure.

What he was sure of was this: Even if he fell on his face before the dance was through, he would rather crawl on hands and knees than depend on his crutches again.

"You can kill me later, and I'll even give you the gun." His hands grasped hers. "But dance with me first."

Her hands were shaking and damp, but so were his. His need for her was too strong. He wanted to hold and love her forever, not just for the duration of a song.

She opened her mouth to speak, but no words came, only a gasp of joy that might have been his name. And then her arms were hugging his waist tightly and he was cupping her face, tracing her tears, and pressing his lips to her forehead.

"You can walk." She was crying openly, clutching at him, moving back to stare disbelievingly at his legs planted firmly on the floor with no crutches in sight. "My God, my God. I can't believe it. My prayers . . . answered."

"We need a wedding dance," he shouted to the band.

"Name your tune, mister," the singer called back.

"'Lady.' By Kenny Rogers." As the piano began the intro, Sol whispered, "Because you're my lady, Mariah."

Taking the lead, Sol drew her close and pressed her against him, then moved with heavy feet, his dance steps an uneven shuffle that felt as liberating as if he had sprouted the wings he'd feared she would spread to leave him behind.

Mariah caught his left hand and kissed his wedding ring. "I love you," she whispered hoarsely.

"Don't ever stop believing in me, baby, or in us. I'm sorry for—"

"Hush." She pressed her fingers to his lips. "Nothing is worth spoiling this." She laid her cheek against his chest as the music played on.

"You're my lady," Sol repeated when the song was over. His voice was rough with emotion and fatigue made his knees shake.

In the silence that followed, they stared at each other as if they were the only two people in the room, in the world. Then a clap sounded from the crowd. It was followed by another and then another until they were surrounded by applause and whistles. They shared a passionate kiss before turning from the dance floor.

With shouts of congratulations, the crowd parted for them. Sol couldn't take his gaze off Mariah, or she him, even though people were reaching out to pat them on the back or grasping their hands for a quick shake.

Many of the people were strangers, but even strangers knew the language of love and rejoiced in miracles.

Nineteen

"Sol! Sol, stop it," Mariah squealed. She squirmed under his tongue, which was busy lapping up the last drop of champagne in her navel. "That tickles!"

"Yeah? Well, just try to run away, now that I can keep up," he growled. Splashing a generous amount of the bubbly liquid onto her abdomen, he made her squeal some more.

"You're wasting the champagne." She giggled when it rolled down her stomach and trickled between her thighs.

"It's never been put to better use, lady." As he set about tracing the liquid's path, Mariah decided Sol definitely had a point.

Sighing languorously, she reached down to sift her fingertips through his hair. Snowflakes drifted past the window, and the glow of the moon reflected brightly off the land covered in white. Candle flames danced from all corners of the room, gilding sprays of mistletoe and other signs of Christmas drawing near.

Sol kissed his way up and she embraced him,

wondering if any woman had the right to feel so complete, so blissful. Their bed shifted as he drank from the bottle and then passed it from his lips to hers.

Feeling delirious with delight, Mariah gave in to silliness and gargled, then swallowed.

"Mrs. Standish, I am shocked." Sol took another swig and imitated her. "You are no lady."

"Not tonight, I'm not. Hand over that bottle, and—oh no, last drop."

"Got another bottle chilling, baby. A marriage certificate coming by special delivery tomorrow is at least a two-bottle occasion. Especially when we waited long enough for most folks to split up and get married again."

"Sure we shouldn't save that bottle to share with Turns? After all, he is flying an awfully long way to make sure we get this one, since the first got lost in the mail."

"Hell no. Not after all his hemming and hawing and losing forms and more craziness going on at his end than sense. I wonder how he'd like it if our positions were switched." After nipping Mariah's neck with a lusty growl, Sol chuckled. "Of course, in our current position, he'd probably like it just fine. Except I'd hate to end a long-standing friendship, so maybe he'd settle for . . . Beth? She'll be here with your parents tomorrow night. Maybe we could make the sleigh ride a foursome."

"We could make it a fivesome by next year if you weren't so hardheaded about me entering school next fall."

"Mariah," he said warningly. "We agreed—no babies, so you can take this year off to study. Finish school fast and open your practice on the farm first. Then we'll see about making the next generation of

Standishes. If we have a few kids, maybe there'll be a natural dairy farmer in the bunch."

"Okay, okay." She sighed, then smiled. After she'd made Sol realize he was the wind beneath her wings, he'd gotten cocky enough to create a fair amount of turbulence. Drawing upon LaVerne's sage advice, she relented enough to make peace while asserting her space. "I've read most of the textbooks, and Hilda's been a wonderful practice patient. Did you know veterinarians have to be even smarter than regular doctors?"

"Hmmm. Seems I've heard you say, it's because animals can't tell you what's wrong with them and people can?"

Laughing, Mariah realized that in her newfound passion for the calling she felt her gift was intended for, she had rambled on about what she was learning. Now that she was sure of herself as an individual and a woman, she no longer hid what she had been born with. In fact, she rather liked showing off to Sol, who was most impressed with her "sexy brain," as he'd put it.

"Besse did not die in vain," she said, suddenly serious. "That's when the idea to become a vet took hold in me. One day, Sol, I'll revolutionize veterinary medicine. I'm going to explore treatment procedures that no one's even thought about. I'm already working on some ideas in my head. You were right—waste is a crime, and I'm giving back to nature what nature gave me."

"That's my girl," he said proudly. "Better yet, that's my wife and my lover. Did I ever tell you how sexy you are when you talk smart? C'mon, baby, whisper some statistics and formulas in my ear. You know how that turns me on."

"*You* turn me on," she murmured, undulating beneath him. "Even more than animal husbandry."

"I *am* animal husbandry, love. After all, I'm an animal. . . ." He bit her neck and tongued her ear before he whispered possessively, "And your husband."

"Well, if it's not the special-delivery boy. Welcome to the neighborhood, Turns."

Turns and Sol shook hands, then discarded that for a bear hug. Holding Sol away, Turns looked him up and down, shaking his head while his eyes grew suspiciously moist.

"Where are your crutches, big man? Last time I saw you they were the only things holding you up."

"Yeah, well, there's a special someone who gave me a reason to get on my feet. I wanted to surprise you."

"Surprise me? First you outwit the Grim Reaper and then you make those damn doctors into a bunch of liars."

"Careful how you talk about doctors around here." Sol wrapped an arm around Turns's shoulder and escorted him to his parents' great room, where Christmas music was playing.

The huge pine he and Mariah had cut down and hauled to the big house, and which the whole family had spent hours decorating, twinkled a welcome. Sol's favorite ornament was a big, tacky one printed with "First Christmas Together"—an early present from Ma and Dad, which was identical to the ones he and Mariah had bought separately, then exchanged with each other.

O'Henry had nothing on them, they'd declared, laughing, while hanging up the three duplicate uglies.

"Smells like Christmas around here, pal," Turns said. "I can almost hear the jingle bells."

"Dad's hitching the horses, so more than likely you're hearing right. Thought we might all go on a sleigh ride tonight to celebrate the season, now that the best of friends is here to share it—and, of course, that long-awaited legal document."

Turns's smile went flat, but Sol was too caught up in the festive spirit to pay it much heed.

"Hey, Mom, Mariah, look who's here! Got a mighty important person for you to meet." As Mariah and LaVerne turned from the tree, Sol said quietly, "You want to know why I'm walking? You're about to meet her. She practically kicked me in the butt when I got off the plane with a chip on my shoulder, held me up when I stumbled, and even when she's nowhere in sight, she's still with me every step of the way. In other words, I'm crazy about her."

"Sol, we need to talk."

"Sure, Turns, lots to catch up on. And heeere she is," Sol announced as Mariah and LaVerne drew near. Sol wrapped an arm around each of their waists. "This is my wife, Mariah, and the other fair lady who answers to Mrs. Standish is—"

"Mrs. Standish, it's a pleasure." Turns tipped his hat, avoiding more than a fleeting glance at Mariah.

"Call me Vernie, Turns. Or Mom, since I feel like you're part of the family, what with you being a household name."

"And I want to thank you, Turns," Mariah chimed in, "for arranging our marriage and doing all the hard work to see that the paperwork was taken care of. I'm sorry for my own holdup. It's more my fault than anyone's for the delay, so don't let Sol give you a hard time."

"*I'll* give you a hard time," Sol whispered softly in

her ear. Mariah snickered and planted an elbow in his side while Turns became strangely preoccupied with the tips of his shoes.

"Eggnog, Turns?" LaVerne was already heading for the punch bowl in the kitchen.

"Uh . . . Mariah, you think maybe Vernie needs some help?" Turns looked at her hopefully while he turned his hat in his hands. "I need a minute alone with your husband."

When Mariah started to leave, Sol tightened his hold on her. "What's the matter?" he said brusquely.

"It's . . ." Turns cleared his throat. "It's about your marriage certificate. Maybe Mariah should go to the kitchen with your mother before we discuss this."

"Mariah's not going to the kitchen, Turns, unless that's where she prefers to be. Anything you've got to say to me can be said with her present." The eggnog he'd had earlier churned uneasily in his stomach. Darting a concerned glance from Turns to Mariah, he asked, "You want to stay or leave?"

"I'm not going anywhere until I know what this is all about. What seems to be the problem, Turns?"

"God, this is bad." Reaching into his breast pocket, he pulled out an envelope. "I was afraid I couldn't say it, so I wrote it down just in case."

Sol took the envelope, practically tearing it in half as he opened it. He extracted a single sheet of typed paper, and holding it between him and Mariah, he read in unison with her.

> *"Dear Sol and Mariah:*
> *Please forgive me. Before you throw me out on my keister, I just ask for enough time to explain. But the long and short of it is . . .*
> *You're not married.*
> *Love, Turns."*

"Not married?" Mariah said faintly.

Sol crumpled the sheet of paper in his hand as if it were Turns's neck he was choking.

"Eggnog's here!" LaVerne extended a Santa Claus mug to their guest.

"I . . ." Turns paused. "I'm not sure if I'm going to be around long enough to drink that."

"Take it." Sol's voice was low but sharp. Mariah flinched; Sol was intimidating to the point of being scary when he got like this. Deciding she could handle him better than anyone else, Mariah decided to quickly intercede.

"Yes, Turns, have some eggnog," she said graciously. "In fact, why don't the three of us sit in the living room and talk about this?"

"I think Dad might need some help with the horses. I'll come back with him later." With that, LaVerne disappeared.

When Sol didn't move, Mariah stood on tiptoe and kissed his cheek. Whispering in his ear, she said firmly, "You've been friends too long not to give Turns a fair hearing. If you won't do it for him, do it for me."

He hesitated, then gave a curt nod. Once they were seated, Sol tightened his arm around her while Turns mopped his brow. "Silent Night" played on.

"Start talking," Sol finally said.

"Okay, but don't stop me until I'm through." Turns took a deep breath, then started talking fast. "When Sol was dying I tried to do my best to give him his final wish. The problem was that a chaplain was nowhere around so I made do with the closest orderly."

"What? You mean some kid juggling bedpans officiated?"

"I didn't have a choice, Sol. And I know I should

have come clean afterward but you were in such a sorry shape, holding in so much anger and ranting about how you should never have gotten married. I knew if I told you the truth then you wouldn't give Mariah a chance, that you'd go from bad to worse if you didn't have someone to think about besides yourself."

"He's right, Sol," Mariah agreed quietly. "You've said as much yourself."

"Why didn't you tell me sooner instead of doing all this backing and forthing of papers and mouthing lip service about the union being blessed by God?"

"Because I figured out Mariah was probably a kid. Sorry, Mariah. I was dead wrong."

"He admitted he was wrong, Sol. Give him a break—"

"I'll give him a break, right between the—"

Turns interrupted. "When she didn't send me her birth certificate, I started getting the picture. But I wanted to buy you both some time—especially you, Sol. That's why I didn't say anything about it missing until you started getting antsy."

Mariah and Sol exchanged glances, then said in unison, "But why didn't you tell us after we sent it?"

"To tell you the truth, I didn't think the 'marriage' would work out. I was trying to give Sol a chance to get back on his feet and at the same time saving him the trouble of a divorce. Believe me, my intentions were good, and I couldn't be happier that I was wrong about things going sour. By the time I realized the two of you were going to make it, I was so deep into this crazy thing, I knew I had to see you both in person to explain. My fear was that Sol would hang up on me if I gave him the news over the phone and never speak to me again. Of course, that's still a very real possibility."

Not married? Mariah blinked while a numb sensation set in and realization finally hit. She was staring at the lapping flames of the roaring fire when she reached for Sol's hand—and grasped emptiness. He'd gotten up to walk toward the fireplace, where he braced his palms against the mantel. The Christmas carol was over, and only the crackle and splinter of burning wood sounded in the absolute silence. Suddenly, he threw Turns's wadded-up letter into the fireplace.

Sol turned. His brow creased into a frown, he stared hard at Turns . . . and then Mariah. Sol shook his head, but his frown softened. His lips went from a thin line to a gentle curve as he slowly smiled. The smile became a grin, then grew to a chuckle, and finally rolled into a resounding guffaw.

Mariah and Turns looked from Sol to each other, their own lips beginning to twitch, though she wasn't sure what was so funny.

"Get your butt over here, baby," he ordered, opening his arms wide. "Your common-law husband needs a kiss."

Mariah was off the couch and in his embrace in a second. When he was through kissing her, and she done kissing him back, Sol motioned Turns to join them. Once he did, Sol wrapped his arms around his two deceivers.

"I guess this means we're still friends?" Turns said hopefully.

"Better than friends. You're going to be my best man. You know, this is just about the most ironic joke and the kindest twist of fate life ever threw in my direction."

"It . . . it is?" Turns asked.

"Don't you get it? The whole thing's a scream. The truth is, if you or Mariah had been truthful from the start, I'd be miserable, she'd be miserable, and we wouldn't have a wedding to plan starting this very minute."

The unexpected sound of stomping boots and animated laughter rushed in from the front door.

"Mariah, honey, guess what the wind blew in all the way from Mobile, Alabama?" LaVerne said.

"Looks like we won't even have to mail out invitations," Sol said, striding forward to shake hands and exchange hugs with his in-laws. "Turns, Dr. Tom and Nita Garnet. And Beth. If she looks familiar, it's because you saw her—never mind. We've had enough explanations, at least until I've taken care of an important detail."

Mariah, still stunned by all the revelations and Sol's switch of moods, was the only one who didn't move as everyone formed a circle around her and Sol.

She felt his hands, so warm and strong, cup her face. His smile faded and he stared down at her with purpose and limitless love. Covering his hands with her own, she felt the unity of skin to skin, of wedding rings that bespoke their unbreakable bond.

"Mariah," he said solemnly, "will you marry me?"

Epilogue

A roaring fire blazed. Poinsettias sparkled with glitter from all over the farmhouse's living room. Snowflakes drifted outside the window in a serene dance of nature. It was, Sol thought, about the most beautiful setting for a wedding he'd ever laid an eye on.

Standing in front of the Christmas tree with Turns and Beth on either side of him, Sol watched Mariah slowly walk up the hallway of this home that had seen joy and tears and life with three generations of Standishes. He counted himself damn lucky to have that heritage to share with Mariah. She wore his mother's wedding dress, which had been her mother's and her mother's before her.

He met Mariah halfway, and amid Nita's and LaVerne's sniffles, Tom's and Herbert's nods of approval, and the rustle of wedding finery, the ceremony commenced.

The minister spoke of love and miracles, truth and trust—all the things that bound Sol and Mariah and which they had asked to be a part of their vows. So caught up in the radiance that was his wife, Sol was caught off guard when Turns nudged him.

"Sol," the minister repeated, "do you take this woman, Mariah Garnet, for your lawfully wedded wife?"

Heedless of tradition, Sol drew back her veil and stole the wedding kiss, then said firmly, "I do."

"By the power vested in me, I now pronounce you husband and wife. You may now kiss—"

"That's been taken care of." Sol hoisted his wife into his arms and strode through the living room. The murmurs of friends and family blended with LaVerne's sudden playing of the wedding march on the piano.

"Sol, what do you think you're doing?" Mariah squirmed in his arms, then gasped when he swatted her behind in front of everyone.

"What I've been dying to do since the first day I held you." Stopping short of the door, he captured her lips for a fierce kiss. "I'm carrying my bride over the threshold."

THE EDITOR'S CORNER

What could be more romantic than weddings? Picture the bride in an exquisite gown. Imagine the handsome groom in a finely tailored tuxedo. Hear them promise "to have and to hold" each other forever. This is the perfect ending to courtship, the joyous ritual we cherish in our hearts. And next month, in honor of June brides, we present six fabulous LOVESWEPTs with beautiful brides and handsome grooms on the covers.

Leading the line-up is **HER VERY OWN BUTLER**, LOVESWEPT #552, another sure-to-please romance from Helen Mittermeyer. Single mom Drew Laughlin wanted a butler to help run her household, but she never expected a muscled, bronzed Hercules to apply. Rex Dakeland promised an old friend to check up on Drew and her children, but keeping his secret soon feels too much like spying. Once unexpected love ensnares them both, could he win her trust and be her one and only? A real treat, from one of romance's best-loved authors.

Gail Douglas pulls out all the stops in **ALL THE WAY**, LOVESWEPT #553. Jake Mallory and Brittany Thomas shared one fabulous night together, but he couldn't convince her it was enough to build their future on. Now, six months later, Jake is back from his restless wandering and sets out to prove to Brittany that he's right. It'll take fiery kisses and spellbinding charm to make her believe that the reckless nomad is finally ready to put down roots. Gail will win you over with this charming love story.

WHERE THERE'S A WILL . . . by Victoria Leigh, LOVESWEPT #554, is a sheer delight. Maggie Cooper plays a ditzy seductress on the ski slopes, only to prove to herself that she's sexy enough to kindle a man's desire. And boy, does she kindle Will Jackson's desire! He usually likes to do the hunting, but letting Maggie work her wiles on him is tantalizing fun. And after he's freed her from her doubts, he'll teach her to dare to love. There's a lot of wonderful verve and dash in this romance from talented Victoria.

Laura Taylor presents a very moving, very emotional love story in **DESERT ROSE,** LOVESWEPT #555. Emma Hamilton and David Winslow are strangers caught in a desperate situation, wrongfully imprisoned in a foreign country. Locked in adjacent cells, they whisper comfort to each other and reach through iron bars to touch hands. Love blossoms between them in that dark prison, a love strong enough to survive until fate finally brings them freedom. You'll cry and cheer for these memorable lovers. Bravo, Laura!

There's no better way to describe Deacon Brody than **RASCAL,** Charlotte Hughes's new LOVESWEPT, #556. He was once a country-music sensation, and he's never forgotten how hard he struggled to make it—or the woman who broke his heart. Losing Cody Sherwood sends him to Nashville determined to make her sorry she let him go, but when he sees her again, he realizes he's never stopped wanting her or the passion that burned so sweetly between them. Charlotte delivers this story with force and fire.

Please give a rousing welcome to Bonnie Pega and her first novel, **ONLY YOU,** LOVESWEPT #557. To efficiency expert Max Shore, organizing Caitlin Love's messy office is a snap compared to uncovering the sensual woman beneath her professional facade. A past pain has etched caution deep in her heart, and only Max can show her how to love again. This enchanting novel will show you why we're excited to have Bonnie writing for LOVESWEPT. Enjoy one of our New Faces of '92!

On sale this month from FANFARE are three marvelous novels. The historical romance **HEATHER AND VELVET** showcases the exciting talent of a rising star—Teresa Medeiros. Her marvelous touch for creating memorable characters and her exquisite feel for portraying passion and emotion shine in this grand adventure of love between a bookish orphan and a notorious highwayman known as the Dreadful Scot Bandit. Ranging from the storm-swept English countryside to the wild moors of Scotland, **HEATHER AND VELVET** has garnered the following praise from *New York Times* bestselling author Amanda Quick: "A terrific tale full of larger-than-life characters and thrilling romance." Teresa Medeiros—a name to watch for.

Lush, dramatic, and poignant, **LADY HELLFIRE** by Suzanne Robinson is an immensely thrilling historical romance. Its hero, Alexis de Granville, Marquess of Richfield, is a cold-blooded rogue whose tragic—and possibly violent—past has hardened his heart to love . . . until he melts at the fiery touch of Kate Grey's sensual embrace.

Anna Eberhardt, who writes short romances under the pseudonym Tiffany White, has been nominated for *Romantic Times*'s Career Achievement award for Most Sensual Romance in a series. In **WHISPERED HEAT**, she delivers a compelling contemporary novel of love lost, then regained. When Slader Reems is freed after five years of being wrongly imprisoned, he sets out to reclaim everything that was taken from him—including Lissa Jamison.

Also on sale this month, in the Doubleday hardcover edition, is **HIGHLAND FLAME** by Stephanie Bartlett, the stand-alone "sequel" to **HIGHLAND REBEL**. Catriona Galbaith, now a widow, is thrust into a new struggle—and the arms of a new love.

Happy reading!

With best wishes,

Nita Taublib
Associate Publisher
LOVESWEPT and FANFARE

Don't miss these fabulous
Bantam Fanfare titles
on sale in MAY.

HEATHER AND VELVET
By Teresa Medeiros

LADY HELLFIRE
by Suzanne Robinson

WHISPERED HEAT
by Anna Eberhardt

In the Bestselling Tradition of Julie Garwood

HEATHER AND VELVET
by Teresa Medeiros

A courageous beauty and her sensuous outlaw ignite fires of passion that blaze from the storm-swept countryside to the wild moors of Scotland . . . forging unbreakable bonds of love.

One moment lovely Prudence Walker was living the life of a dutiful orphan, the next she was lying in a highwayman's arms. Wounded in a foiled robbery attempt, and thoroughly drenched from a storm, the dreaded Scot bandit seemed harmless enough. Or so Prudence thought—until the infamous rogue stole her breath and her will with his honeyed kisses, until she felt the rapier-sharp edge of his sensuous charm.

She was everything Sebastian Kerr had ever wanted, but could never have; an impish beauty with amethyst eyes and wine-sweet lips he longed to plunder. But even as he drew Prudence into his embrace, he knew he must leave her. For the gray-eyed highwayman was leading a dangerous double life, one that left no room for love. . . .

Prudence's mouth went as dry as cotton as the lantern flame shed a halo of light over the highwayman's face. His tawny hair was badly in need of a trim. She reached to brush it back from his brow before she realized what she was doing. Snatching her hand back, she inadvertently touched the hot tin of the lantern. She stifled a gasp of pain, telling herself one burn was better than another.

Lifting the lantern higher, she hungrily studied his features. The sun had burnished his skin to a warm, sandy color that nearly matched his hair. His low-set brows were a shade darker. A thick fringe of charcoal lashes rested on his cheeks. Aunt Tricia would do murder for such lashes, Prudence thought. Not even copious amounts of lamp black could duplicate them. His nose was slightly crooked, as if it had been broken once, but its menace was softened by the faintest smattering of freckles across its bridge. A pale crescent of a scar marred the underside of his chin. Shallow lines bracketed his mouth and creased his forehead. Prudence suspected they had been cut not by time, but by wind and weather. She judged his age to be near thirty.

The lamplight played over his mouth like a lover, and Prudence felt her chest tighten. It was a wonderful mouth, firm and well formed, the bottom lip fuller than the top. Even in sleep, the slant of his jaw tightened it to a sulky pout that would have challenged any woman. Prudence wanted to touch it, to make it curve in laughter or soften in tenderness.

She leaned forward as if hypnotized.

"Amethyst."

The word came from nowhere. Her gaze leaped guiltily from the bandit's lips to his wide-open eyes.

*   *   *

Prudence was caught in a trap of her own making, paralyzed not by the accusing circle of light, but by the stranger's eyes, which were the misty gray color of summer rain. She felt like a dowdy moth beating its wings against a star.

"Amethyst?" she repeated weakly. Perhaps the bandit was dreaming of gems he had stolen.

"Your eyes," he said. "They're amethyst."

She blinked. Prudence had no difficulty seeing things close to her, so there was no need to squint now. If she closed her eyes, she suspected she would still see his face, etched indelibly on the slate of her mind. He did not touch her, but she could not move. Poised there in the light, she waited for him to reproach her or yell at her or shoot her. She bit her bottom lip, then loosed it quickly, remembering how her aunt said the childish habit emphasized her buckteeth.

Sebastian studied her frankly, his earlier suspicions confirmed. The girl was utterly lovely. The delicate alabaster of her skin gave her even features a surprising fragility. A nearly imperceptible cleft crowned the tip of her slender nose, and the primness of that nose was belied by a faint overbite that hinted at an alluring pout. Stubby dark lashes framed her violet eyes. The lamplight sought out burgundy highlights in the velvety tumble of her hair.

Sebastian caught a coil of that hair between his fingertips. It was as soft and heavy as it looked. He had forgotten the pleasure of touching a woman's hair without getting powder on his hands. The steady throb of his ankle waned as a new throb shoved blood through his veins in a primal beat.

His eyes narrowed in a lazy sensuality Prudence mistook for drowsiness. "Put out the lamp," he said.

She obeyed, relieved that she had escaped being scolded or shot. Darkness drew in around them. The firelight cast flickering shadows on the far wall.

"Lie down beside me."

Her relief dissolved at the husky warmth of his voice. The darkness shrouded his features, reminding her he was a stranger, with all the dangerous edges of any unknown man met in the seductive solitude of night.

She twisted her petticoat between both hands. "I'm not very tired, thank you."

"You're not a very good liar either." His hand circled her slender wrist. "If I offend you, you may kick me in the ankle. I'm relatively harmless right now."

Prudence doubted he'd be harmless with both legs broken. No man with a mouth like that was harmless.

"I won't hurt you," he said. "Please."

It was the "please" that did it. How could she resist such good manners in a highwayman? After a moment of hesitation, she stretched out beside him, her arms and legs as rigid as boards. He slipped an arm beneath her shoulders in a casual embrace, and her head settled in the crook of his shoulder more easily than she would have hoped. Rain pattered a soothing beat on the thatched roof.

"Have you no family to worry over you?" he asked. "Won't they be frantic when you haven't returned?"

"I'm supposed to say yes, aren't I? So you'll hesitate to throttle me lest they should burst in."

He chuckled. "Perhaps you're not such a bad liar after all. Have you heard rumors of me throttling women?"

She thought for a moment. "No. But a friend of my aunt's, a Miss Devony Blake, claims you ravished her last summer. It was the talk of every picnic and ball for months. She swooned quite prettily each time she told the horrid tale."

"Which I'm sure she did," he said curtly, "in frequent and exacting detail. What do you think of this Miss Blake?"

Prudence buried her face against his collarbone. "She hasn't a brain in her silly blond head. It was more likely that she ravished you."

"So only a girl without a brain would ravish me?" His fingertips traced a teasing pattern on her arm. "Tell me—will this aunt of yours be wondering where you are?"

"She had gone to a midnight buffet when I went out. Perhaps she'll think I snuck out for an illicit tryst." Prudence smiled at the improbability of the thought.

Sebastian did not find the idea amusing. His arm tightened around her shoulders. "Did you?"

"Aye, that I did." Again, she mocked his burr with uncanny accuracy. "To meet the bonniest fellow betwixt London and Edinburgh."

Sebastian's ankle started to throb again. "Your lover?" he asked quietly.

"No, silly—my Sebastian."

Hearing his name spoken in his mistress's adoring tones, the kitten lifted his head with a drowsy purr. Sebastian took advantage of the distraction to slide his hip next to Prudence's, feeling unaccountably elated at her words. The kitten deserted the crook of his elbow and climbed onto Prudence's chest by way of her stomach.

"Fickle beast," he muttered.

He reached over to pet the animal, and his hand found the kitten's silky fur at the same moment as Prudence's. Their fingertips brushed, and she laughed breathlessly.

"It seemed such an ordinary morning when I awoke," Prudence said. "I had my bath. I put up my hair. I ate my prunes and cream." Her voice sounded odd to her, more like Devony Blake's than her own. "If anyone had told me I would be having such an extraordinary adventure by nightfall—I mean, lying in a highwayman's arms—I would have thought them insane."

He pulled his arm from beneath her and propped himself up on his elbow. "And if anyone had told you a highwayman would be kissing you?"

She swallowed. "I would have judged them a madman, lunatic, bedlamite . . ."

Her voice trailed off as his fingers entwined with her own. His head bent over her, blocking out the meager firelight, and he touched his wonderful mouth to hers. She shivered at the unfamiliar heat. He tenderly brushed his lips across hers, and with each tantalizing pass deepened the pressure, melding his lips to hers as if they had always been meant to be there. His mouth was every bit as smooth and firm as she had fancied.

"Delicious," he murmured as he pressed tiny kisses along her full bottom lip and each corner of her mouth.

No one had ever called her "delicious" before. Prudence thought she might swoon, but then he might continue to kiss her. Or worse yet, he might stop. She quenched a sharp flare of disappointment as he did just that.

His lips brushed her eyelids. "Close your eyes." His hand cupped her chin; his thumb slid sleekly across her bottom lip. "And open your mouth."

"I—I don't know," she said, her words coming in nervous spurts, "if anyone has suggested this to you before, but you have an inclination toward bossiness. It is a character flaw that might be remedied if—"

Before she could close her mouth, he swooped down and gently caught her lower lip between his teeth. Her gasp was smothered by the sly invasion of his tongue. His hand tightened on her jaw, holding her mouth open until she hadn't the will or the inclination to close it. Then his fingers slipped around to the nape of her neck in a velvety caress. His tongue swept across her teeth and delved deeper. Prudence thought she might die when she felt the shock of its warmth against her own. She should have been repulsed. Decent women did not kiss this way. But somehow having her mouth taken and stroked by this man was not repulsive, but captivating. Her own tongue responded with a tentative flick.

The highwayman groaned as if in agony, his strong fingers twisting in her hair.

She pulled back, suddenly remembering his wounded ankle. "Am I hurting you?"

"Aye, lass. You're killing me. And I love it."

In the Bestselling Tradition of Amanda Quick

LADY HELLFIRE
by Suzanne Robinson

A lush, dramatic, and touching historical romance, LADY HELLFIRE is the captivating story of a cold-blooded rogue whose dark secrets have hardened his heart to love—until he melts at the fiery touch of a sensual embrace.

After braving the perils of the wild frontier, there wasn't a man alive that Katherine Grey couldn't handle . . . or so the reckless spitfire thought . . . until she found herself on British soil, and in the presence of the devilishly disturbing Lord Alexis de Granville, Marquess of Richfield. Dangerously attractive, mysteriously tormented, he ignored her, disarmed her, enticed her. But Alexis had too many women in his life, and Kate vowed she'd never be just one more. . . .

To Alexis, women were for solace, to be used as they had always used him. Yet lovely Kate refused to play the game. One moment she scandalized him with her brash American manners, the next she seduced him with her lush lips and flame-colored hair. Worst of all, the tempestuous wench touched his faithless heart. Now, in a castle beset by treachery, Alexis will do anything, fight anyone, to make her want him as much as he needs her. . . .

Afternoon was fading when Alexis went in search of Kate again. He'd spent the intervening time trying not to think about her. He'd never tried not to think about a woman before. Never had to. It didn't work, and so he'd made the mistake of allowing himself to remember that she'd smiled upon that colossal sausage-wit Cardigan.

As soon as he did, he felt as if ants were swimming in his blood. He wanted a fight, and not just any fight, but a fight with Katherine Ann. Katie Ann. Mouthy, presumptuous, succulent Katie Ann. He found her in the kitchen garden stabbing at weeds with a trowel.

"Why are you digging in the dirt, Miss Grey?"

The blade hit a rock. Dirt flew in Kate's face and she swore.

"Hellfire. Do you have to sneak up on people and shout at them?"

Alexis studied one of his immaculate white cuffs before letting his gaze shift to the dirt on Kate's small nose. He grinned when she sputtered, discarded the trowel, and began wiping her face with the apron she wore to protect her dress.

"I asked why you are playing in my cook's garden."

"I used to take care of our garden at home. I miss it."

"Are you finished?" He held out his hand without giving her a chance to say no.

Taking Alexis's hand, she rose. "I guess I am." She placed her hands on the small of her back and leaned backward, groaning. "Oh, my. I haven't gardened in a while. What are you laughing at?"

"I don't think I've ever seen a lady pull her arms back and stick out her chest before. Not in my whole life." He laughed again at the confused look on her face and glanced pointedly at her breasts. "Your posture, Katie Ann. Gentility and maidenliness seem to be lacking across the Atlantic."

She scooped up the trowel and poked him with it. "I don't need you to tell me what maidens should or shouldn't do or talk about, Alexis de Granville. And stop grinning at me. And don't call me Katie Ann. My father is the only one who called me that."

"He must have been a brave man." He captured the hand that held the trowel. "A brave man to raise such a lightning storm of a daughter as you, Katie Ann."

He let her snatch her hand away. She rounded on him, and he watched her ire grow. She was mad enough to spit bullets. Her cheeks were flushed, her eyes bright with unladylike wrath. And he felt more alive than he had in years. Alexis couldn't help laughing again.

"You ass," she said.

"Please." He held up both hands in mock protest. "My sensibilities, Katie Ann. I shiver to think what body part you'll mention next."

"You can take all your body parts and go to hell," she said. She turned her back on him and marched across the garden to the kitchen door.

"Come back, Lady Hellfire," he called after her. "You've yet to speak of the most interesting body parts."

It was on the fourth day that she gave up all hope of understanding Alexis de Granville. She'd taken great care in selecting a hiding place in which to read. He'd found her when she'd gone to the Red Drawing Room, the Cedar Drawing Room, and the armory. This time she took refuge in the Clocktower.

The tower was a fourteenth-century construction with over fifty rooms. It stood just inside the massive barbican, the outer fortified gate house in front of the drawbridge. She selected a deserted chamber stuffed with medieval furniture and sporting a fireplace big enough for a man to stand in. What attracted her was the tall, diamond-paned window that let in the morning sunlight. The brightness streamed in and reflected off the white stone of the tower walls.

She dragged a heavy walnut chair over to the open window, then curled up in it and opened the book she'd brought with her. Her view was of the turquoise sky and a single, thin wisp of a cloud that hung like a bride's veil spread by the wind. What sounds there were came from the stirring of the pages of her book when a breeze caught them. She gradually sank into a world of bright light and beautiful words.

"Aaarrrroooof."

Kate jumped. Her knee hit the arm of her chair, and she yelped. There was a scuffling of paws, then the door to the chamber slid open under the weight of Iago's shoulder. The spaniel bounded forth. He sprang and landed with his front paws on Kate's thighs and barked again.

"Iago!" she heard Alexis call, his voice sounding too innocent.

"Damn," she said, and shoved Iago off her lap. "Go away, doggie."

Iago burrowed his head in her skirt. She got up and began pulling the dog by his collar.

"Come on, Iago. If you don't get out, he'll find me."

She was pushing on the beast from behind when the marquess stepped into the room.

"There you are, old fellow," he said. "Kate, this is a surprise."

"I don't see how. He's hunted me down three times now."

"I know. Odd, isn't it? We set out on a walk, and he comes to fetch you right away."

Iago barked, batted his paw at Alexis, and bounded out of the room.

"Now where's he going?" Kate asked. She tried not to sound annoyed.

The marquess threw up his hands in mock disgust. "I don't know. Sometimes I think he consorts with pixies so he can disappear and appear at will. What are you reading?"

Before she could stop him, he snatched the book from the chair where she'd left it.

"*Le Morte d'Arthur*," he said. "I didn't think you'd read such romantic stuff. Knights and damsels and chivalry. Do you like romance, Miss Grey?" He didn't wait for her to answer. "Shall I read to you?"

Again he didn't wait. He started reading while leading her back to her chair. Kate frowned at him as he sank down at her feet. He was so close he almost touched her knees. She'd never had a man read to her. She was so surprised that he would want to, she let him. At first she was uncomfortable, but the sound of his voice lured her into forgetfulness. It was a low, soft voice infused with feeling and vibrancy, and it set her insides tingling in the strangest way.

The tingling made her forget the words. She listened to the sound of his voice alone. When he rested his arm on the seat of her chair, she moved so that he would have more room.

He glanced up at her and smiled. Without looking at the book, he recited. "'Then Sir Mordred sought on Queen Guinevere by letters and sounds, and by fair means and foul means, for to have her to come out of the tower of London; but all this availed not, for she answered him shortly, openly and privily, that she had liefer slay herself than to be married with him.'"

Kate looked down at him. Inside she felt a small shiver of excitement. His voice wove a spell. It shot out magical tendrils that combined with the cool, bright air, the smell of old wood, and the warmth of his body, suffusing her in charm. She paused, balancing on an enchanted strand of faerie web between his spell and her own caution. He was looking up at her still, but his eyes changed. They became liquid metal. She started when he put his hand on hers and lifted it to his lips.

"If I were Malory," he said, "I would have Guinevere have fire-light hair and skin like the glaze on ancient porcelain. She would have earth-brown eyes and little hands that disappeared when I covered them with one of my own."

His hand slid over hers. She looked to remark that it did vanish, and when she did, he was there. His mouth came up to meet hers, and she opened her own as if it were the only thing to do.

It couldn't be helped. She wanted to kiss him, so she did.

In the bestselling tradition of Sandra Brown

WHISPERED HEAT
by Anna Eberhardt

From the moment Lissa Jamison first saw Slader Reems, she knew they belonged to each other. The tender-hearted boy sparked her youthful infatuation, but the wild and wounded young man he became lit a blazing hunger within her. Then came the night Slader was torn from her, when love was devastated by betrayal.

Holding Lissa was Slader's sweet agony on his last night of freedom. Remembering her was his sole comfort during the five years his body and soul were caged. Finally free, he's back in town to reclaim her—and everything else that was taken from him.

Slader insists Lissa belonged to him body and soul, but she knows she can't surrender to the man who could destroy her, yet who still makes her burn for his touch. She has rebuilt her life on the ashes of the past, guarding her heart in a passionless prison, and only a wildfire of longing can break her free. . . .

The jeans riding low on his hips were kept on by a whisper of a promise. He let the screen door slam, annoyed that Melissa was still sleeping, annoyed she'd disappointed him . . . *annoyed*. Lissa . . . he'd idealized her for so long, and now he had to come to terms with the real woman she'd become while he was in prison. She must really like the rich life, he thought. She hadn't stirred yet, and from the position of the sun, he'd wager it was past noon.

He opened the refrigerator and popped the cap on a beer, chugging it down to slake his thirst. What he needed next was a pair of scissors, he decided, to turn his hot jeans into a pair of cutoffs. Remembering the sewing kit that was always kept in the upstairs hall closet, he went to see if it was still there.

Reaching the upstairs hall, his gaze wandered to the master bedroom.

The door was open.

Though he tried to ignore it, he found himself drawn to it . . . the forbidden beckoning like the pages of an open diary. Without consciously willing it, he discovered himself standing in the open doorway.

The four-poster bed in the middle of the room was rumpled; the sheets were twisted. His gut twisted as well at images of Beau and Lissa there.

He heard the shower running, then saw a bathroom had been installed adjoining the bedroom, making use of the area where a small storage closet had been.

Feeling sneaky, but overwhelmed by curiosity, he ventured into the bedroom. The closet door was open. He winced when he saw Beau's clothes hanging next to Lissa's. Too intimate. It was a symbol of the reality of their marriage. He was on his way to close the door of the closet, to shut out the offending sight, when something on top of the frilly dressing table caught his eye. There, next to an open black jet-beaded box from which a string of pearls spilled, was one of the two wooden toy cars he'd made for Lissa for the Christmas that now seemed so long ago.

Both wooden cars had had wheels that worked. He rolled this one absently back and forth on the glass-covered surface. The car had changed with time; there were a few nicks and scratches, and it had darkened with age. It was incongruous next to the things on the dressing table.

Had Jamie been playing at her feet while she'd been dressing to go out one evening and left it there when she'd picked him up to put him to bed? He rather liked the idea of Lissa's son playing with the car he'd made. He thought of Jamie as Lissa's son, not Beau's.

He didn't hear the shower stop while he was lost in the world of "what ifs."

He saw her in the mirror when he looked up. She'd moved to stand beside the four-poster bed behind him. She was fluffing her hair with a pale pink towel. Obviously she didn't realize what the raising movements of her arms were doing to her breasts, so free and mobile beneath the white floor-length terry-cloth robe she had on. She'd tied the robe hastily, and it gaped just a bit to reveal a subtle flash of cleavage. She looked every inch a lady, and the slightly gaping robe gave hint she was every inch a woman.

The fragrances of soap and shampoo engulfed Slader. The herbal scent was sweet and familiar. Everything had changed in five years except the soap and shampoo she used. And his feelings.

He turned to face her.

She was still damp from her shower, as clean as he was dirty. They stood there . . . opposites.

He wanted her. He wanted her on the bed she shared with Beau. He was the one who loved her and worried about her. It should have been him, not Beau.

He walked toward her.

She didn't move.

She just stood there looking at him. Into him.

When he stopped in front of her, they were both breathing shallowly, the pupils of their eyes wide and soft. In the silence an alarm clock ticked forebodingly.

She watched a droplet of sweat slide down the stubble of his jaw and settle in the hollow of his neck. A cloud moved over the sun, throwing the room into shadow.

Slader reached out soundlessly and pulled the sash on her robe. Lissa's only reaction was an involuntary indrawn breath. The robe hung, still closed, damply molding her body. The pink towel she'd been drying her hair with slipped from her hand to the floor as she continued to stare at him.

Watching.

Waiting.

Barely breathing.

He looked into her wide soft eyes, challenging what was happening between them; his eyes showing his wonderment that she was making no move to stop it.

Her only perceptible movement was the flicker of her eyelashes as his hands reached toward her again. His forefinger rigid, he eased the robe open, his callused finger grazing the smooth swell of her left breast, leaving a dusty trail on her slick skin.

He waited.

Holding her gaze, he moved his finger to the right, his warm, dusty finger trailing the damp rise of her right breast. He pushed the robe off her shoulders, revealing her body fully to his thirsty stare.

He looked at her slowly, carefully . . . as if he were memorizing, as if he were afraid he was looking at something precious he would never be able to see again.

As she watched him his eyes gave nothing away. Not even when her nipple responded to his touch.

Melissa felt her knees weakening, desire following in the wake of the path his gaze traveled. Stepping back reflexively, she felt the edge of the bed against the back of her knees. She looked up at him expectantly.

Mesmerized, she watched as he took another step forward, pinning her against the bed without touching her. Her breath caught in her throat at the hunger in his eyes.

Her eyes drifted closed.

But Slader didn't lay her back across the bed.

When she opened her eyes, she saw that Slader had won his battle for control. He looked at her for a long moment, then turned and left the room. As quickly as it had begun, it was over.

Not one word had been exchanged between them.